Painting Their Portraits in Winter

Also by Myriam Gurba

Dahlia Season: stories and a novella

Painting Their Portraits in Winter

short stories

Myriam Gurba

Manic D Press
San Francisco

Pa' mi ruca, Adriana. Most Unique and Best Eyebrows por vida...

The author gratefully acknowledges *Anthropoid Collective* for originally publishing "Hummers" in slightly different form. "Even This Title is a Ghost" originally appeared in slightly different form in *Sweatsuits of the Damned* (Eli Coppola Memorial Chapbook, 2013).

 Published by Manic D Press. For information, contact Manic D Press, PO Box 410804, San Francisco CA 94141 www.manicdpress.com
Printed in Canada   ISBN 978-1-933149-90-5

Front cover artwork: ©Can Stock Photo Inc./lineartestpilot
Back cover author portrait: Arcelia Garcia de Alba
Design: Gadzooks!

Contents

"It doesn't just *look* like no one lives here. No one *does* live here."
"And Pedro Páramo?"
"Pedro Páramo died years ago."
—Juan Rulfo, *Pedro Páramo*

How Some Abuelitas Keep Their Chicana Granddaughters Still
While Painting Their Portraits in Winter

It was December and it was just girls — Mom, my sister Ixchel, and I
— staying in the damp house where Mom grew up in Guadalajara. When
Mom was the age I was that winter, ten, Mexican death was prettier, slower,
and more public. Mom would laze in front of her house, in a strip I guess
you could call a front yard, in front of her mom and dad's bedroom window,
dangling her chicken legs off the stone bench, a spectator. A breeze might
shiver the vines wriggling around the window and bring the smell of
cemetery flowers. Mom would hear a signal, horseshoes clacking. She'd
look right and see a gelding chosen to do his job because of his color, black,
clopping up the avenue, chugging towards her block. The horse would
near houses that were twins of the kind Mom lived in, two-story rectangles
shaded with mold, loquat trees by the driveways, vines climbing wherever
they chose. The animal would be yoked to an old-fashioned funeral carriage
that truly honored death, its lace-gilded windows giving Mom a chance to
appraise the size of the coffin — baby, child, or full — and then, once the
carriage was past, Mom could observe the ribbon, or ribbons, of mourners
in black outfits, weeping, yawning, scratching their necks, wringing one or
both fists, adjusting their balls, breastfeeding, moving their feet and taking
care of their living bodies' needs on their way to bury someone.

The days of funerals with horses were gone and Mom's mom, Abuelita,
would walk Ixchel and me up this avenue, along the high cemetery walls
painted with murals portraying the days of death and horses. We'd be on
our way to get our midweek groceries. Abuelita's food store wasn't like our
American ones, indoors with waxed floors and waxed fruits and fluorescent
lights. Her market was an outdoor rally of vendors who set up shop in a
park circled by rangy pines. Abuelita would haggle with men and women,
threaten to walk away to get the best deals on garlic and tomatillos, and
when she bought papaya, I'd carry it like it was a baby and cradle it to our

next stop, the butcher shop. There, Abuelita would tell the man dressed in blood and cotton how many knuckles and how much tripe.

Abuelita carried our food home in plastic mesh bags with plaid designs. Waddling along the cemetery murals, she looked how a Mexican grandmother should, like a tropical babushka. Four feet, eleven inches of old lady. Rolls of diabetic weight held in place by a handmade dress. Silver hair cropped short by her own scissors. A yarn shawl flapping like a cape. Uneven knee-highs growing further apart and hand-sized feet jammed into orthopedic shoes. Arms hanging thick as tamales, and calves and shins pulsing with subcutaneous leeches, varicose veins.

Abuelita filled her dining room with caged birds she had bought and found. She'd feed them bits of shortbread, and Ixchel and I learned to feed them by watching, mashing stale cookies and sprinkling fleshy crumbs over the wires, spreading fairy dust. Amid these birds, at the dining room table, Ixchel and I worked on the packet of assignments the school district had issued for our absence. We read textbooks and little stories and computed math problems to birdsong.

Abuelita had a TV in her bedroom that she said we could watch, but TV was weird at Abuelita's. It was dubbed, so Ixchel and I didn't like it. We felt uncomfortable watching the Smurfs in Spanish. It seemed wrong, so in our down time we took to shadowing Abuelita. As an artist, she availed herself of our presence. No man would guess seeing her walk up the street that Abuelita was an artist, and no man would guess that my sister and I were subjects worthy of art. Abuelita thought we were. She turned us into creations.

Abuelita tricked us; we didn't realize she was doing it. She tricked us into keeping frozen so she could make something out of us. She told Ixchel and me, "Sit," and sat us in two uncomfortable wood and twine chairs with calla lilies painted on their backs. Posing on the seat that would bedevil my pompis for days, my spine to the front hall's long, white wall, I learned Abuelita wasn't just a decent painter—she had a Mother Goose talent, too. She could take a story like *Hansel and Gretel*, and make it ten times juicier, as gruesome as death is long.

In the middle of the tile floor, Abuelita would be seated on an equally uncomfortable chair, wearing a red and white checked smock. She'd drag her rough easel closer and push the canvas resting on it an inch to the left. Her spectacles would slide to the end of her pearl nose. Her squishy hands would squirt colors out of long tubes and onto a palette she held like a Parisian, its paints would stink deliciously, and Abuelita would poke a blob — umber, sienna, whatever — with her brush tip. Look at us across the tops of her rims.

"Listen," she'd say. And then, in Spanish, she'd speak in a tone that conjured the same feelings as *once upon a time*. Ixchel and I surrendered.

"There was an old lady who lived in Guadalajara, a nice old lady with a small house and a stand where she sold tamales. Hers were good, but they weren't the best. Many others in the city sold similar tamales, so the woman made enough to live decently and not want for the necessities of life."

Abuelita's brush stroked back and forth. Its movement and her voice and the humming light bulbs and the skittering roaches placed us under hypnosis.

"She was a typical old lady and her little house was nothing special. Like some old ladies do, she opened her home to the children of the street, the orphans and the indigent, inviting them inside for something warm to eat, for tamales. She told the children that if they helped her with her small business, she'd feed them and give them a place to sleep. This offer appealed to many, and they worked hard for her because she kept her word; she fed them and gave them a warm, dry place to sleep. Soon, forgotten children from all over Guadalajara began appearing at the doorstep of the old lady who'd won fame for her generosity and kindness. The children would cross her threshold, and some wouldn't emerge. She told her neighbors that they were very, very busy. Inside the house, they were cooking and cleaning and doing chores for her, making meal and grinding chiles for the sauce that goes into the tamales."

Abuelita stopped to swirl pink, white, and mustard. Her vigor shook her body, making her glasses' chain quiver.

"A divine aroma began to pipe out of the old lady's house, and this odor seduced the people of the city. The citizens of Guadalajara flocked to her tamale stand and began to buy so many tamales from her that often she ran out before the day was through. She opened more stands around the city, and the orphans helped her with their operation. People became crazy for the tamales, it became a mania, and those that partook said the meat she was using was the softest, most tender meat they had ever had. People would beg her for her secret, but when they would ask her, she would simply shake her head back and forth, smile and answer, 'No. If I were to tell you my secret, I would spoil it for everybody.' One day, at the tamale cart that was posted on the street where she lived, a customer bit into one of his purchases and screamed."

Abuelita paused. She looked Ixchel and me in the eye and grinned. "He had bitten down on something hard." Abuelita shook her brush handle at us. "He reached into his mouth to pull out what he thought might be a pig bone and pulled out something long and thin." Holding her brush as though it was a teacup, Abuelita hoisted her pinky into the air. "It was a finger, the small one from the end of the hand, with its tiny fingernail still attached."

Glee made me squeal. Ixchel moaned.

"Don't move!" Abuelita warned.

I readjusted my pose. Ixchel gulped.

Abuelita continued, "The old woman's tamale business had gotten so popular she had become sloppy in her butchering and improperly diced one of the orphans! A mob formed outside her home, they pounded her door, and when they finally battered it off its hinge and spilled inside, they could not believe what they saw: children held captive in a small back room, nourished by the meat and bones of other unfortunate creatures until they were fat and ready to be slaughtered. The children were lethargic and bloated and nude, bones, hair, and skulls littering the diabolical space where they'd been held prisoners.

"After the terrible discovery, the mob went to get the woman and lynch her. They wanted justice but night was falling, and as they stormed the streets looking for her, she was nowhere to be found. The only trace of her was an owl that came to perch in her doorway at sundown. This bird let out a hoot, as if it were bidding farewell, turned tail, and flew into the night sky, in the direction of Tonalá, the land rumored to be the home of many witches. She was never seen again. My mother," she paused, "was from Tonalá."

Abuelita stared at us.

"Another…" I suggested.

For the next two weeks, Abuelita fed us yarns that let her paint us. There was one about a one-eyed lecher who lured Indian girls into his house to "clean." He'd been disfigured by an accident that took his wife and his eye, and because its socket dried up like a mouth with no teeth, nobody wanted to go near him anymore. Perverted appetites took fuzzy root in the guy's psyche, and he promised girls the chunky gold ring he wore on his left hand's fourth finger if they'd stay with him for a week and get a poor widower's house in order. Without fail, at the close of her second afternoon with the cyclops, his newest housekeeper would bolt into the street screaming, crying, and ranting. She'd tell everyone about the unbelievably nasty things the one-eyed guy had asked her to do, some involving the eye socket, but telling didn't matter. There'd always be a desperate girl willing to go back inside.

There was this other story about a lady who wrapped a knife in her rainbow-striped rebozo and set off to kill her sister's lover, a man who also happened to be her husband. Like Paul on the road to Damascus, a winged visitor appeared to her as she speed-walked through the woods. The visitor was a dark-skinned angel dressed in a white cloak, and in its threads glowed a vision of her fate if she continued her afternoon journey: her husband would survive the stabs, and he would live to taunt her from outside prison walls. The vision vanished, the angel swooped back into the sky, and the would-be murderess plunged to her knees and sobbed. She was heartbroken that her knife would not be making her husband's throat smile.

Abuelita's shortest tale was about a little girl who disobeyed her mom. She went on strike like a syndicalist, refusing to do chores till she got paid, and was exiled to her room for her defiance. Kneeling on the floor with her doll, pouting, she felt muggy breath on her shoulder. The striker turned and faced a black German shepherd with maraschino cherry eyes. His stare showed her what damnation felt like, and she never disobeyed her mom again.

And then there was the story of the nuns. Abuelita was mastering the final touches on our portrait when she told it. Ixchel was squirming, casting her eyes left, at the front door, checking for our aunt's shadow. She'd promised to take us ice-skating inside a pyramid. I, too, was looking forward to going ice-skating in a pyramid, but I wanted Abuelita's stories more.

"The nuns lived in a beautiful convent," Abuelita said, hooking us, "not located inside the city but on the outskirts. The grounds were beautiful, and the nuns lived there, behind a tall brick wall that hid everyone's view of what went on inside. The people who made deliveries to the convent said that behind the fence were palatial living quarters and sumptuous grounds where sweet smelling rose gardens bloomed all year round."

Abuelita dabbed our sister portrait with rosy paint, licked her top lip, and continued, "During the revolution, extravagant convents, like this one, were destroyed. The goal was to give the land back to the Mexican people — peasants, its rightful owners, farmers who would sincerely work the earth. The revolutionaries knew that the world inside the convent mirrored the world outside it, and those who came from wealth continued to enjoy it within the cloister. Novitiates who came from lower classes continued to suffer as they would have elsewhere, practically enslaved, forced to wait hand and foot on the nuns who came from prestigious families.

"When the revolutionaries arrived at the convent, they wanted to destroy it. They hated the church and accused it of hypocrisy, and they heard that some men from the old regime were hiding there. The revolutionaries stormed and ransacked the nunnery, searching for men, and found them, hiding in the chapel belfry. These men were taken as prisoners, marched down the stairwell, lined up along the gate, and shot. Next, the nuns were paraded into the courtyard and told to strip beside the flowerbeds. The revolutionaries were animals: they raped the prettiest first. When they were finished, they hung the ugly ones, one by one, from the trees."

I became pop-eyed. I wasn't sure what "rape" meant but Abuelita had given me plenty of leads.

"The convent was to be dismantled and the land it had been built upon redistributed to local villagers. Peasants arrived. Their hands and hatchets tore down the nunnery, and from its walls, they harvested infants' skeletons. Almost every wall held the bones of at least two newborns, and as people dug in the garden outside, a similar discovery was made; a dozen tiny skeletons were yanked from the earth.

"The peasants surmised that the skeletons in the walls were products of the nuns' indiscretions with anonymous clerics. The babies in the garden were another story. The peasants believed those babies were the reason the convent had hosted the daughters of the wealthy, the daughters of tequila barons and the biggest thieves of all: men who worked for the government. These girls would stay with the nuns for seven, eight, or nine months and then be sent back home, svelte and rested. The nuns would dispose of their beautiful bastards in the garden. The mulch from their flesh and bones was what enabled the convent's flowers to bloom all year long."

Ice Capades

Dad and Mom had left for a bullfight, and since they didn't want to be bothered by their children while they watched beef die, they left us at Abuelita's. I thought I was going to have to watch TV or get Abuelita to tell me more rape fairytales, but then we finally saw our tía Ofelia parking her beige Lincoln Continental by the corner hamburger stand, Hamburguesas Garfield. I don't think Hamburguesas Garfield was named after the president. I think it was named after the cat. Ofelia unchained Abuelita's gates and let herself inside.

"Put on sweaters," she told us. "We're going skating."

I set down the cookie I was about to crumble. I tasted anticipation. It tasted like chewing a pencil before a spelling test.

I'd watched tarded (leo- and uni-) people skate on TV during the Olympics. I'd also watched New Yorkers in earmuffs skate Rockefeller Plaza by that 'roided-out Christmas tree someone stole from the woods. I'd never experienced ice-skating in vivo. Growing up fifteen miles from the California shore, my community suffered from beautiful weather year round. This had often made me feel deprived. Being a winter sports virgin somehow made me feel less American.

The closest we came to snow was frost bedazzling the lemon, orange, and avocado trees' leaves in our front yard. The manmade lake down the street never froze. I wanted to live in a cold climate where I could throw a Donner Party.

Guadalajara's ice-skating rink sat inside a replica of a Mayan temple, and this faux ruin was actually the shell of the Hyatt hotel. Ofelia drove us there in her Continental and led my cousins, Rosita and Ganzita, my sister, and me to its entrance. Her slingback black heels clacked against humid pavement. There was nothing Mayan about the ground floor. In its center, the rink breathed steam. Hardly anyone skated on it, a couple of losers on butter legs. I'd own the ice, manifest my red, white, and gringa destiny, become an Ingalls. Stores with names that make you feel poor saying them — Hermès, Gucci, Armani — lined the pyramid's walls. Ofelia was a whore for French and Italian fashion, that was the real reason she'd been so generous. The snob wanted to shop, and she slobbered at the sight of sharply lit window displays.

We followed Ofelia to a booth and rented skates from a short man in a Dodgers cap. Ofelia glanced at the boutiques as we sat on dark benches threading eyelets, lacing the skates up our shins. I double-knotted my bow and watched Ofelia lift her Rolex to her nose job.

"While you guys skate, I'm going shopping. I'll be back in an hour. Don't go anywhere." Seduced by the promise of intensely expensive retail therapy, she floated away. The stink of Chanel No. 5 went with her.

I shuffled to the edge of the self-healing black floor. My feet scooted onto the ice, and my blades slid across it. It felt similar to roller-skating, and that I was bomb at. We had a roller rink in town at the fairgrounds, and I could skate to Salt-N-Pepa's "Push It" till my toes bled. I couldn't skate backwards but I could skate squatting, in the position I imagined female slaves in the American South had probably been forced to give birth in. America, the horror. Sometimes, when I skated squatting, I imagined a fetus half-dangling out of me. I watched my breath puff out of my mouth. Ghosts. Raising two fingers in a backwards peace sign, I pretended to smoke. All the sophisticated people I knew smoked and pounded tequila shots, and I skated faster, feeling Alpine. Canadian. I knew I had it in me to play hockey. I was American. I was superior to all these mango-eating fuckers trying to glide on the ice. I moved my arms back and forth in imitation of the athletes in Chapstick commercials. I lapped everyone over and over, grinning as I passed them. In spite of the block of ice that buoyed me, I sweated. My calves and hamstrings burned. My perm frizzed. I would get fitter than the teddy bears doing aerobics on my sweatshirt.

I glanced and saw Ofelia leaning on the edge of the rink, Gucci bags dangling from her forearms. I tasted sadness; it tasted like bird shit. The stores were shutting. I could see shop lights blacking out and girls pulling metal cages around storefronts. Ofelia's bony, manicured hand motioned for us to come. We skated back to the benches and unlaced. We traded skates for tennis shoes and put them back on.

We walked out of the pyramid and into the ethnic armpit of night. Ganzita and Ixchel and I climbed into the backseat. Rosita rode shotgun. We rode across town. Strands of white lights glimmered along the avenues. Pedestrians bustled with shopping bags and tacos. The smell of carne al pastor, car exhaust, and unrequited longing blew at us through the open windows. A red light made us stop before entering the roundabout. A statue of Christopher Columbus fondling a globe would've cast its shadow across us had it been noon. I looked to the lane left of us. The cars seemed strange. Nobody was in the driver's seats. Nobody was riding either. Everyone in the Continental realized this emptiness at once. In unison, our heads scanned the lanes. To the right, another car ghost town. Everyone had abandoned the intersection and there we were, a car full of Chicanas, Mexicans, and Gucci bags.

Men came running up the lane. One wore white jeans. One wore tan jeans. One wore blue jeans. All wore leather jackets. They carried AK-47s. They looked ugly enough to be extras or character actors. The men surrounded a gray sedan and beat their hands and rifles against its doors and windows.

"Open the doors, you fucking bitches!" screamed the man with squinty eyes.

There was a car with people.; one car with two women in it. A youngish woman sat in the driver's seat, looking from man to man. A woman in the backseat, maybe her mother, looked from man to man. Her face wore an expression that was both terrified and uncertain. I glanced at their door locks to see if they were up or down. The little knobs were down. Their sedan was their cage. The older woman grasped rosary beads in her left hand. The younger woman threw her hands in the air and wrung them. She wailed, but from where we were, it was only a mouth moving. No voice.

"Bitches!" the men screamed. "Open the doors!"

The men seemed ready to crack open windows, drag the bitches into the street, and slaughter them at Christopher Columbus's feet, a human sacrifice for an Italian god.

"Mommy," said Rosita. "Drive!"

"But the light is red," said Ofelia.

"Go!" we all urged, and Ofelia sped through the unusually long red light.

"Get down!" shouted Ofelia. Everyone did except me. I stared through the rear window as the men, the women, the rifles, and Columbus shrank. Cousins muttered prayers to assorted saints, and after two blocks we spotted a motorcycle cop with gut flopping over his belt. He wore aviator shades. He sat as comfortably as a fart in a bathtub. He might've been sleeping.

"Tell the policeman!" we screamed.

Ofelia pulled up to the cop. Rosita rolled down the window. Ofelia screamed, "There are men with machine guns attacking women by the statue of Christopher Columbus!"

The policeman's body didn't shift. He said, "Thank you." He was waiting for us to leave.

Ofelia's heel hit the gas. We sped away. Adrenaline kept me high as we passed the park where Dad's parents had met and the city's best churro shop. We passed the cemetery and came to Abuelita's neighborhood. Ofelia parked the Continental at the curb and I burst across Ixchel's lap, out of the car, and rattled Abuelita's gate.

She speed-limped outside to unchain it. I tore past her and into the front hall. I darted into her bedroom and flew onto her bed. I leaned over to switch on the TV. I flipped channels, looking for the news or newsflashes.

My grandfather, wearing a three-piece suit accented by a pocket square, shuffled into the room. Turning to look at him, I caught a glimpse of myself in their mirror. My cheeks were rosy. My eyes bulged. My perm was out of control. Abuelito moaned, "Why are you so excited, m'ija?"

With breathless pride, I explained, "On the way here, we saw men with machine guns attack women by the statue of Christopher Columbus!" I felt I was the harbinger of news, NEWS, and I knew that what I'd seen was the kind of thing that was supposed to be on TV. "I'm trying to find the news report about it!"

17

Abuelito chuckled. He shuffled to me. His liver-spotted hand reached for my head. It patted my tropically induced 'fro. I smelled perfume that was not Abuelita's.

"That's not going to be on TV," he said. "It's not going to be anywhere." He creaked away, chuckling.

I didn't believe Abuelito. I flipped through the TV stations for hours but the asshole was right. There was nothing about men with machine guns attacking women at the statue of Christopher Columbus. Since nobody put it on the news, I guess it didn't matter.

E = MaChismo^2

Abuelito interrupted me as I was updating my Facebook status. He'd been dead for over a month. I could sense he wanted me to shut off my uncle's computer and go to sleep. He didn't want me to be sleep-starved for Abuelita's death.

In life, Abuelito was a vain misogynist. In death, he became a mostly invisible ghost.

This must drive his ghost crazy. In *Pedro Páramo*, the seminal novel by Abuelito's nemesis, Juan Rulfo, Mexico's most notable surrealist, the vain don't inherit the earth. Ghosts do.

Ghosts colonize the imagination. Imaginations are the ultimate haunted houses.

In the haunted house where I was Facebooking, I'd heard the doorknob turn. I'd turned to look. I quit breathing while I waited for one of my uncles — the nice one, Miguel, or the asshole, whom I'll just call "the asshole" — to appear in the doorway. Neither did. Nothing appeared in the doorway. A feeling of supernatural narcissism engulfed me. Abuelito was announcing himself.

"Go to bed," he whispered into my mind.

I felt terrorized. I wanted to obey Abuelito's ghost, but that meant shutting off the lights. I shut off the computer. I got up and walked from the bed to the door. I poked my head into the hallway to see if there was anybody alive outside.

Darkness and the smell of moldering newspapers greeted me. That's the smell of Abuelito. When he was alive, he worked primarily as a publicist. He claimed to have named most of the places in Guadalajara. For example, there is a place named Plaza Del Sol, Shopping Center of the Sun, and Abuelito explained to me that while walking through it, as it was being built, a sun-shaped light bulb lit up over his head. Gestalt.

"There is a lot of sun here!" he exclaimed. "We shall call this place 'Plaza del Sol'!"

If Abuelito discovered the sun, Rulfo discovered the moon.

I came back to bed and sat on the bedspread. I looked at my uncle's carpentry books lining the brown shelves and a trophy won by a hairless dog, a xoloitzcuintli, Samson. I looked at Abuelita's painting of my uncle Miguel, and thought that in it, he looked a little like a fag. He's not.

I was sitting at the dining room table, listening to birds squawk. I could smell the ground beef Abuelita was stirring around a pan on the stove. Miguel was sitting at the table with Abuelito and me.

Abuelito smoothed his hands across his vest and pocket square. He slid a fedora onto his head.

"M'ija," he said to me. "How many children do you want to have when you get married?" He smiled paternally. Mexican paternalism evokes the scent of chorizo.

"None," I answered. "I'm never getting married."

It was the first and only time I saw Abuelito look astonished.

"Why?" he asked in a tone of voice people usually reserve for the question *How did the accident happen?*

"Because I am a feminist," I answered. I was twelve years old.

Abuelito burst out laughing. He leaned over and petted me on the perm.

"Don't think so hard, m'ija," he said and left to see his mistress, taking his chorizo scent with him.

When Mom sat down Abuelito at the dining room table and told him, "I want to go to college to study chemistry," his answer was "No. Women get married, they go to the convent, or they become secretaries. I'll pay for you to go to secretarial school but not university. That's a waste of an education."

Years later, he paid for his mistress's daughters to go to university.

Perhaps, his chorizo actually did evolve.

Abuelito unlearned his peasant roots at the seminary he attended with Rulfo. There, priests imbued him with fake class. They taught him how to write well enough. He became interested in poetry but not for the muse's sake. Abuelito saw poetry as a vehicle for his chorizo. Seduction. Narcissism. His sonnets smell of pork, moldering newspapers, secretaries' vulvas, and clichés.

In grade school, Mom read one of his poems — a love poem about a thorny rose — in an oratory contest. She lost.

Somewhere in my imagination, Abuelito is sitting at his dining room table. Because my imagination is cold, below eighty degrees, for a Mexican's, Abuelito wears a beanie, scarf, and earth-toned serape. A purple scab dots the bridge of his nose. His gray moustache is its own animal; it's about to jump off his upper lip and run away. Go join the other moustaches and hamsters that live together in a hole in the wall.

In front of Abuelito, on a placemat, rests an unpublished manuscript. A dedication appears under the title. I can't quite read it.

In a voice that's more moan than groan, he asks, "Have I told you about when I was in seminary? With Rulfo? Mexico's greatest novelist? Well, in my opinion, and I am a writer, too, Rulfo doesn't deserve that title. His writing is about dirt. Worms. Ghosts. Bricks. Bad weather. Things that don't honor anybody. And it doesn't make any sense, you don't even know who's talking or telling the story. Rulfo was, to put it politely..."

Abuelito's ghost keeps talking. Jealous ghosts never shut up.

Mom attended private schools. One was near the orphanage where Abuelita lived with her sisters, and Mom was so bony that as their teacher was walking them through the yard, she didn't notice Mom had veered left while her classmates continued forward. Mom slipped between the iron fence bars and came face to face with downtown Guadalajara. It became hers.

Wearing her uniform, she strolled around the plaza and its gazebo where young men and women congregated at night to flirt. Women swam in circles around it, and if a guy liked her, he brought her a flower and saved her from the orbit.

Coins clinked in Mom's vest pocket. She scurried to a man manning a white cart. She told him, "A mango with lime and chile, please."

From his cart, he lifted the fruit impaled on a stick. He grabbed taut citrus, held it over, and squeezed. Clear juice bled. Droplets caught sunlight and looked like sparks. The vendor grabbed a bottle, held it over the mango, and red dabs fell, coating the marigold meat. He handed the spear down to Mom, and she thanked him with a thin-lipped grin. Juices dripped down her fingers and wrist while she nibbled, and she wandered along rosebushes, gnawing, wasps carrying a masonic tune nearby. Mom grabbed the mango with her other hand and flicked her juicy fingers at them. Her potion sprinkled them. Instead of attacking her, they sailed away.

Mom looked up at the broken clock crowning the gargoyle-laden Governor's Palace. The Mexican flag slumped above it. Supposedly, an ancestor had aimed his rifle at the clock and shot it in the face during a major or minor war over something like land or god, and his hole had remained. His hole reminded everyone that violence was always ready. His hole also reminded everyone that violence makes holes. Mom tossed her spear and mango stone at the rose bushes. Surprised bees evacuated. They droned for their queen's comfort.

Mom skipped along cobblestones, thrilled to be ditching. Everything looks more decadent when you're ditching, peanuts and cigarettes taste better, too, and Mom skipped to the Garden of Letters. Writers set up shop there, in rosewood shade and under brick arches. At their card tables, they spread blank paper and whittled pencil points with paring knives. They wrote for people who couldn't and could. They wrote for full-blown illiterates and crappy communicators. A day's work could include an eviction notice, a lilac-scented love letter, and an essay about Sancho Panza's supporting role in *Don Quixote*.

Mom blocked the sun with her hand to see if her dad was at his usual post. She saw someone else working there, a man without her father's honker or patriotic mustache. Mom crept closer and meandered the periphery of the square, scouting for her father. Not seeing him among the scribes, she turned to leave. She headed in the direction of a bookstore when her father's profile appeared against a window displaying three mannequins dressed as brides.

Mom sped up her walk and followed a few yards behind him. She tailed him along the row of cantinas where the city's most ground-up hookers worked and Death hung out — she's a creature you should save your last kiss for — and then Mom followed Abuelito around the orphanage and beyond, to a row of buildings hundreds of years old with hand-of-Fatima door knockers.

Standing on a stone step, Abuelito grabbed one of the hands. He rapped its fingertips against wood. Chocolaty door swung open. A petite former secretary stood at the threshold. Abuelito leaned in and kissed her on the lips. A baby girl with her father's nose straddled the lady's secretarial hip.

I opened my eye. It was not confronted by pussy. That onslaught only happened in Tío Miguel's room.

If Abuelito was hogging the bathroom, the only other toilet you could use was Miguel's, and to earn relief you had to journey through the labyrinth of pornography that filled his bedroom.

Even on his toilet, Miguel treated you to muff. On the door across from his commode hung a life-size poster of a lady in a see-through blouse splaying herself, Georgia O'Keefing you as things shot out of your own flower. I minded all the pussy but, at the same, part of me welcomed it.

Hopping out of bed, I left Mom and Ixchel and made my way down the hall where Abuelita had painted our portraits. I padded into the space where the piano nobody played sat against a moldy wall. Nearby, Abuelita's caged birds blinked, twitched, and called.

Abuelita was standing at her round kitchen table, holding a dainty machete. She hacked into an infant-sized papaya, halving it, exposing seeds that were black pearls capable of making papayitas. My appetite was turned on by the fruit's aroma: part feet in July, part bubblegum, part cotton candy, a dash of crotch. What a feminine breakfast.

Abuelita looked from the black pearls to me. She gasped and then pointed her machete at my face. "What happened to your eye?" she asked.

I wasn't sure. It hadn't bothered me much when I'd woken up, but now that Abuelita mentioned it, I reached up and touched my blind spot, my right eye. My fingertips rubbed skin swollen smooth and shut. The flesh pulsed with uncharacteristic warmth. My blindness was running a temperature.

"Before you eat," said Abuelita, "go show your mom."

I left Abuelita and her fruit behind. I returned to our room. I knelt beside Mom's twin bed. I reached for her shoulder. I shoved it.

"Mom," I said.

She made noises that might scare you if you were alone in the woods.

"Mom," I repeated.

She made more of those noises, but also groaned, "What?"

"Abuelita says you have to look at my eye."

"Why?"

"I think it scared her."

Mom opened her eyes. She looked at me but didn't flinch. "Get me my glasses," she said.

I walked to the corner desk, grabbed her glasses with the big squarish lenses, and delivered them to her veiny hands. She slid the glasses on and examined me.

Her expression changed from curious to concerned yet revolted. "Something bit you in the eye," she said.

I scratched the heat. With the warmth and the slit and the swelling, it was not unlike scratching myself, the Georgia O'Keefe between my legs.

"Stop scratching," said Mom.

"But it itches."

"You'll go blind," she said. Isn't that what they tell people who constantly touch themselves for fun? So that I'd be obeying Mom, I slapped my eye instead.

On our way to the clinic, in the backseat of Miguel's VW bug that he chauffeured Abuelito around in so that he could give lectures about his dear co-seminarian Juan Rulfo, I scratched. My eye drooled pus that mingled with the grime under my fingernails. Together, these ingredients formed a fertile slime I could've sowed papaya seeds in. I could've sprouted vines from my fingertips. Squash blossoms. Pumpkin patches. Gophers could've burrowed there. Hobbits, too. My middle finger, a Middle Earth.

Mom turned to look at me. "I told you to quit scratching your eye."

"But it itches."

"Think about something else."

I thought about the time a distant uncle had asked me if American farts smelled differently than Mexican farts. Somebody had cut the cheese in his living room, and he was sniffing the air, trying to deduce the cheese's nationality. Cheddar or panela? Maybe I had farted. I couldn't remember. I had felt embarrassed. Later on, in private, I'd tested my farts to see if there was an invisible difference, a distinctly Yankee odor. I'd detected none.

I scratched my eye again. Pus slobbered onto my fingernails.

A doctor wearing a white coat over a blue guayabera so pale it was almost snow asked, "What happened?"

My good eye stared at him.

"I think something bit me in the eye," I explained.

As his hands grabbed hold of my face while his fingers gripped my eye socket, pulling open the taut slit that wanted to stay shut, he asked, "Where are you from?"

"California… What does it look like?"

"It looks like something bit you in the eye."

I imagined the offense. I had probably fallen asleep sniffing my fingers (that was my habit) and with them curled against my nose, a mosquito attracted by my smell —as attracted to me as I was attracted to the papaya because of her smell; maybe to the bug I smelled like the United States of America, like hamburgers, hot dogs, potato chips, female vice presidential running mates, and long lines at Disneyland — made my eyebrow her landing strip. Her visionary diet forced her to ignore my cheeks, shoulders, ankles, and groin. This mosquito wanted to taste what I saw.

Kneeling on my eyelid, fantasizing about blood banks, she plunged her proboscis beside an eyelash follicle and slurped. I figured this mosquito might have also sucked from the woman down the street who sold awesome pozole out of her living room. She might have also gotten drunk off the blood of witches with AIDS. Maybe she was descended from mosquitoes that had sucked from historically important Mexicans, like the guy who started the Mexican war for Independence or the eighty-three Mexicans who got squashed fighting the French in the Battle of Puebla. These are the Mexicans to whom American beer companies owe it all. Happy Cinco de Mayo, assholes! Maybe this mosquito had tasted my dreams. I often suffered a nightmare that I had to watch my mother, father, brother, and sister be executed. I decided that my blood tasted like peanut butter and jelly sandwiches with the crusts still on.

"How do you like your president?" the doctor asked.

"They're all the same," I answered.

The doctor let my eye slurp back shut. He turned and began giving Mom directions for how to administer my eye medicine. I reached up to scratch.

"Don't touch your eye!" he and Mom chorused.

When they turned to resume their conversation, I lifted my nails to my eye and scratched till I drew tomato juice.

Mom was on top of me. There was nothing sexual going on. It was the opposite. I was screaming.

Her knees held me still, and her right hand pried my eye open. She held the bottle over it and squeezed. I could see the blur of the bottle, and the descending drop and, reflexively, my eyelid tried snapping shut.

"No!" screamed Mom.

The medicine hit my eyeball. Sizzle. I felt the howl come out of me and fill the room with unnecessary desperation. The dose was two drops.

"I'm sorry!" screamed Mom as she pried my eye open again.

Two days and twelve drops later, Miguel drove us to the airport where several years later, a Catholic bishop would be gunned down... accidentally. We were there to pick up my dad and brother. We stood, herded behind wooden and metal barriers, till we saw the rest of our family. Then we screamed.

"Hi!" I yelled.

Dad kissed and hugged Mom. He turned from her, looked down at my sister and me, and recoiled.

"What happened to you?" he asked me.

"A mosquito bit me in the eye," I said.

Dad stared at me for a bit, smiled to himself, and then hunched his shoulders. He let half of his face palsy. He pointed his performance in the direction of baggage claim. Taking my hand, he limped and said, "Let's go find my bags, Quasimodo..."

Lambada

Were you as confused by AIDS as I was? In Spanish, AIDS is SIDA, which sounds fertile: "Don't move: I'm going to plant some SIDA in you." In English, the syndrome sounds helpful. When I'd hear people talking about it on TV or see headlines about AIDS in newspapers and magazines, I'd wonder, "A plague of help?"

The threat of AIDS made me want to avoid assistance. Help could kill me.

My cousin Andrew did not die of AIDS, but a Samoan did help him die. This Samoan rocked Andrew's world. He grabbed Andrew's handsome head, thumped it melonishly against Southern California concrete, and scrambled his egg.

Hours later, doctors drilled holes into Andrew's head to relieve swelling.

A little while after that, Andrew turned acoustic. His mom, my Aunt Teresa, Dad's oldest sister, let doctors unplug her youngest son.

Dad made us get into the minivan, and he drove us to the east of LA suburb where Aunt Teresa was having Andrew's funeral. I was secretly stoked. I was going to get to miss school *and* see an actual dead person. Up until that point, I'd only buried a dead hamster. This hamster's ghost had visited me. It floated through my bedroom, by the bunk beds. I whispered the hamster's name, and that was its cue to vanish. It came to me that once and ceased visiting. Hers was not a serial haunting.

Standing at the altar, I looked down. I'd imagined Andrew would look smashed. He didn't. All the pieces of his face were where they belonged but he looked as if he was sleeping incorrectly. When you sleep, your eyeballs are supposed to vibrate against your eyelids. Andrew's stayed still. Your chest is supposed to rise and fall. Andrew's stayed stuck. I got as close as I could to Andrew's coffin without climbing inside. I stared at his eyelids. Something underneath them turned their texture lumpy, mashed potatoey.

My cousin Nancy bumped her shoulder against mine.

"After Teresa turned off his life support," she whispered, "she had somebody scoop out his eyes and donate them." I imagined a nurse standing by with a melon-baller. "Somebody out there has Andrew's eyes."

I looked out the church doors. Sun beamed down on a silvery hearse waiting at the curb. I wondered, *if I bump into the stranger who's got Andrew's eyes, will this person still be a stranger? Will they be part Mexican now?* I tried to do the math. Andrew was a quarter Mexican, since his mom was half, and depending on what the stranger was, Andrew's eyes could be the missing piece that completed the stranger's Mexican-ness or the thing that sullied the stranger's whiteness.

I sensed that the recipient of Andrew's eyeballs was probably white. Andrew had green eyes, like Teresa, Grandma, and me. Unripe, mossy, 7-Up bottle verdant.

I checked out my cousin. He was wearing a light gray suit. His complexion was like the wax fruit my piano teacher kept on her coffee table. His coffin gleamed long and smooth as a forty. Cotton balls were jammed into his ears. These leaked embalming fluid that oozed down the corner of his jaw line and trailed down his neck onto his pillow.

The back of Andrew's head felt like a taboo. The idea of what it looked like titillated me. Was it smashed? Were there holes? Could I put my fingers in them and bowl?

Teresa loomed at the foot of the coffin. Her height converted non-believers: Chicanas tall enough to play in the NBA do exist. She had the same amount of body fat as a Virginia Slim. Lunchbag-colored skin wrapped her high cheekbones. She was wearing a pencil skirt and a blouse with a depressed bow tied at her chin.

A guy dressed like *Miami Vice*-goes-Goth sashayed up the pews, past a grotto hosting a big-ass statue of Saint Christopher. The guy turned at the doors and came to us. He threw his head against Teresa's chest.

"Grrrl," he growled. He clutched at Teresa's bones. "I'm so sorry for your loss."

"Who is that?" I whispered to Nancy.

"You don't remember him?" she whispered back.

I shook my head.

"That's Rudolph. Tío Carlos's son. He's our cousin. He's a faggot."

The faggot part explained why he was wearing clear braces and foundation. From his breast pocket, Rudolph pulled a coral handkerchief. He blew a gust of boogers into it. The boogers sounded wet but cheerful.

Something tapped my shoulder. I turned to see what it was. Mom stood behind me.

"Tell your cousin goodbye," she said.

I returned my eyes to Andrew's face. "Goodbye," I told it.

I glanced left. I glanced right. Everybody was absorbed by the unique grief that comes with losing somebody at sixteen. I knew it was my chance to make a memory.

I reached into Andrew's coffin. My fingers touched his. I appraised them. They felt chilly, stiff, and anti-climactic, like omens of my future attempts at compulsory heterosexuality.

Nancy and I sat side by side in a pew to the left of the altar. A priest was talking. Everybody was listening or weeping. I stared at the fag in black.

Our cousin Penny, Andrew's big sister, was reaching for her cane. She stood and hobbled up the altar steps. She stationed herself behind the pulpit. She started to read from a paper somebody had set on the stand for her in advance.

"Do you know why she walks with a cane?" Nancy whispered to me.

"Because of scoliosis surgery," I whispered back.

Nancy shook her curls. She whispered, "Because her boyfriend fucks her in the ass."

I stared at Penny's boyfriend. He was the white guy with a mild pompadour sitting in the front pew. He was wearing a red V-neck sweater with white monogramming. I tried to imagine him ruining Penny's spine via her rectum. My mental conjurings made it so that I turned deaf to Penny's eulogy.

People found it moving though. They were weeping and their voices were cracking, as if they were entering a puberty brought on by grief. Penny hobbled back to her seat. I watched Dad. The experience of tragedy tensed his body. Made it seem less Mexican. More Polish.

Pallbearers wheeled Andrew's coffin towards the doors. Everybody rose to watch. I wondered if, when I died, would I also be handled like groceries? That's how they loaded his coffin into the hearse. Loading him expressed how he was a thing, a thing that you loaded and unloaded. Mourners milled in the parking lot, figuring out who would caravan with whom. Mom turned to tell me, "Come on."

I said, "I'm going with Nancy."

Mom glanced at Nancy. Instead of looking her in the eye, she looked her in her hairpin chola eyebrows.

"Okay," said Mom. "See you at the cemetery."

"Can we ride with you?" Nancy and I begged our faggot cousin.

Grinning, he answered, "You can ride my Mercedes, girls," and I got excited because I caught his reference. It was to Pebbles' song, "Do You Wanna Ride My Mercedes, Boy?" We followed him to his shiny, black turd. Nancy climbed into the front seat. I climbed into the back and scooted to the middle seat. My baroque perm minimized visibility but I didn't care.

Rudolph pushed his sun visor down and flipped open its mirror. He squinted at his reflection. With his index finger, he poked at lesions caked in peachy concealer, trying to rub the makeup smooth again. I grinned at him. His jaundiced eyes locked with mine. I folded my hands in my lap. I was ready.

"Buckle up, bitches," he said. "We've already got one dead body on our hands. I don't need two more."

Nancy strapped herself in. I buckled my lap belt and pulled it tight. I was riding an endorphin high and feeling sexy. My hair was big. I was wearing nice black clothes. No man had ever called me a bitch with such pizzazz. It felt good.

Rudolph turned his key in the ignition, and the German engine did its thing. The radio screeched Bobby Brown's "My Prerogative" and Nancy and I sang, "They say I'm nasty, but I don't give a damn. Gettin' girls is how I—"

"Nancy!" snapped Rudolph. "Change the station. I don't wanna hear that whiny-ass nigga talk shit."

Punching buttons, Nancy got rid of Whitney Houston's future beard. She station surfed. We tailed cars with yellow FUNERAL stickers on their windshields. Our caravan merged onto the freeway but we turned into a gas station. Parking at a pump, Rudolph ordered, "M'ija, hand me my glove."

"Me?" I said.

"Yes," he answered in a girl-on-her-period tone. "It's under my seat."

I bent down, groped, and felt fabric. I pulled free a white glove. I handed it to him.

"Thanks, bitch."

Wearing the single white glove, Rudolph walked to the cashier's bunker. He pushed cash through a thick window's mouse hole, turned, and minced back.

He paused near the door to my left and unscrewed the gas cap. He turned, yanked a handle, and shoved in the nozzle. While fuel spat into the tank, he checked himself out in the tinted window, smoothing down flyaways that were escaping his hairdo.

Bell chimed. Rudolph put the nozzle back in its crack and poured back behind the wheel. After unpeeling his glove, he handed it back to me. I replaced it.

Nancy got back to work DJing and Rudolph said, "Leave it, leave it: This is my jam!" He rapped along to Neneh Cherry's "Buffalo Stands" and when it faded to commercial, he proclaimed, "Grrrrl! Neneh Cherry has some mean titties on her. Shit, I'd even fuck her!" He winked at me through the rearview mirror. "Wanna know who else I'd fuck just to say I fucked her?"

"Who?" I asked.

"Diana Ross." He shivered. "And all those fish in that Madonna video."

He was outing himself. The merpeople in Madonna's "Cherish" video were mermen.

I blurted, "Are you gay?"

Rudolph convulsed. His hysterics made the Mercedes swerve.

"Bitch," he said and paused, "I played with Barbies."

Nancy laughed. I giggled, too. It felt safe since Rudolph made it seem fun and natural to have been a child with homosexual tendencies. I wondered if Rudolph was gay enough for AIDS. Help.

Rudolph hit a dip and started talking shit about the city of L.A., how its potholes had done a lot of damage to the chassis of his car, he was going to sue but he got over his rage quickly, equating potholes to blowholes, and he returned to the mermen from Madonna's "Cherish" video, how he would find a way to do them, he would find a hole, a gill, something, and as we pulled into the cemetery, I glanced at the mausoleum, where skeletons were turning to dust in drawers.

Rudolph parked at the tail of our caravan, in the part of the graveyard where the ground swallowed the recently deceased. We got out. So much sun greeted us, Death couldn't keep it down. I stepped onto lawn.

Rudolph whispered, "Oh my god, lookit my fucking sister."

"Hey!" she screamed. She jogged across graves. Her mustard hair bounced and her mustard shirt was knotted at the waist. A black mini-skirt swaddled her biscuits and her doughy legs poured into mustard stilettos. Her knees were scowling. Her heels stabbed loose dirt and sank.

"Ah!" She waved her arms. "Help! They're pulling me down! They're pulling me down!"

I pictured the deceased reaching for her heels, able to see the hairless piglet between her legs.

"Grrrrrrrrrrrrrrrrrl!" Rudolph lyrically proclaimed. "You look like a mothafuckin' bumble bee."

His sister stuck out her arms. She fluttered her hands and said, "Bzzzz."

I think she was on drugs.

Dad was standing near Andrew's grave. A Saint Francis of Assisi statue was watching over the burial, holding a serene expression. Dad motioned *come here* with his hand. I jogged over dead people while saying *I'm sorry* to them in my head.

"Get in the van," said Dad. "I don't want to see them put your cousin's coffin in the ground."

"But I wanna say goodbye to Nancy and Rudolph!"

"We don't have time. Get in the van."

Dead children horrify Dad. He won't watch movies where children get strangled, dismembered, or tossed off of cliffs. He's sensitive, but I know that at funerals with mariachis, he has been known to whoop, scream, and lambada till the cows — and my mother — come home.

Death was killing time down the street from the orphanage. Her gender was inescapable, especially for her victims: infinitely, infinitely, infinitely female.

Occasionally, she came out when the sun was out but that was mostly to admire her work from the night before. She had been wandering the dirt boulevard and was crouched beside a man who'd kissed her under black sky. His face, contorted by a mystic stare, now looked up at baby blue. Death smiled. She pulled her rainbow-stripes-against-black rebozo around her shoulders. She breathed onto the contorted facial expression she'd created.

"Ahhhhhhhhh…"

The corpse could almost smell her breath. Brittle roses and pork bones. Ladybug urine and monarch butterfly cocoons. Cacti candies and coffee-stained dentures. Bloody underwear. Cinnamon. Accidental mummies. Slaughterhouse sinks.

Her colorless face tilted up. Her pupils dilated, replacing her irises. The toes of her Victorian boots poked out from under her ankle-length ruffle skirt. Embroidered stags pranced around her blouse's neck. Her black braids wound into donuts on either side of her head and woven into the strands were tiny white flowers plucked in hell, stillborn baby's breath.

She enjoyed kissing the life out of drunks. It was easy. She enjoyed killing children. That was even easier. Stumbling down the powdery street, runaways from the orphanage would spot her sunning herself near a donkey or smiling at lunatics arguing with mosquitoes. She'd give the runaways the kindest smile they'd seen in a lifetime, and their hearts would crack open a little. A hairline crack in that child-size gold locket was all she needed.

Her serenity and bread-white teeth seemed so trustworthy, and like stray kittens rediscovering human warmth, they crept to her with hope.

Their skin made her smile. Once their hands touched, she walked them behind the cantinas, along homes with chocolaty doors with rusty hand-of-Fatima knockers, towards the cemetery behind the paupers' hospital. Nameless people got tossed into mass graves there, and the heat and humidity melted them into human bread pudding.

As an orphan would catch a whiff of the cemetery flowers and that unique dessert, Death would turn to watch. She held her breath as her orphans lost their moisture, shriveled, became husks, and turned into crunchy brown calla lilies. They crumpled into little versions of her, little deaths, and she held their brittle hands, amazed that she had the power to turn a child — everybody's hope for everything — into fine, fine ash that wind could blow across a straw mat.

Their father drove the car towards the orphanage. His daughters — Faith, Charity, and Esther — watched the cantinas, hookers, and donkeys go by. A servant held the baby, Rose.

"Where are we going?" Faith asked her father.

"On a vacation," he lied.

He'd been fighting with their mother about not getting enough, and after she'd left that morning, to go to a client's house to take her measurements, he'd told their daughters, "Grab whatever you feel like you can't live without for the next couple of... days." Esther had grabbed her mother's mother-of-pearl combs. Charity had grabbed a blanky she liked to sniff. Faith had grabbed Rose. Their father herded them to his sedan.

They were cresting up the hill from which the orphanage exuded shame. Founded by a bishop when the country was still Spain, the facility looked like the bastard child of Versailles and the Alamo. Its ramparts overlooked the red light district. Sparrows preened on its dome. The sight of parents placing children on its stone steps and running downhill offset the place's palatial quality.

The sedan pulled up to the entrance. At the foot of the steps, a mother with a baby secured to her chest by a rebozo paced. The stones burned her bare soles but whatever psychic agony she was going through numbed her to the heat. The car idled near her.

"Out of the car!" the father yelled. The pacing woman gave a start.

A matron with a bob haircut counted the girls as they spilled out, "... three... four..."

Her hands hung at the pockets of her gray smock. The father strutted to her. He handed her an envelope. She reached for it, and he pressed it into her square hands.

"This is for my daughters," he said. "Don't, I repeat, don't let their mother see them or you will lose your job. My daughters live here now, and they don't have a mother. My daughters get their own room. They will eat food I send. Tutors and teachers will come give them private lessons. I will send them gifts that are to be delivered straight to their room. I don't want them playing with disgusting children, and I don't want them getting worms, dysentery, or head lice. Understand?"

The matron nodded.

He turned, bent, and kissed each daughter on her third eye. The servant handed Rose to the matron. With tears in her eyes, the servant scrambled back into the car.

"See you later!" he called to his daughters and got back behind the wheel. He pulled away, coasting downhill.

The matron thought, *Now I can buy a razor!* She peered into the cash-stuffed envelope. She thumbed through the bills. They felt as smooth as her sideburns were going to feel.

The pacing woman stared at the matron. She felt like shit. She had nothing but a baby to press into the woman's hands. As if to remind her of this, her baby shook the seedpod she was clutching. It went *tsa, tsa, tsa.*

The woman turned and swung her arms as she stomped downhill. The thought, *I wonder if I'll ever get hungry enough to eat her,* came to her. She shook her head, trying to shake the thought out, but when you try to shake ugly thoughts from your head, you give birth to more. *I wonder who would taste better,* she thought, *a very young person or a very old person.* She shivered. Her stomach growled.

From the entry of a billiards club, Death watched her. She smiled. Death knew what she'd been thinking. She could hear her appetites.

Death said, "Excuse me." The mother quit stomping and looked.

Death continued, "I know what you were thinking about doing, up at the orphanage. I saw you, and there's no shame in wanting your child to live in a place where it will be warm and fed, and have brothers and sisters to play with."

Death gave a smile as warm as goat stew. Death delighted in the tears this brought to the mother's eyes. The mother gave Death a crumpled smile.

"Can I hold her?" asked Death.

A tear scooted down the mother's cheek. She handed her baby to Death.

Death took her into her china arms and held her, and breathed that weird potpourri that she'd breathed onto the corpse. She and the baby looked at each long enough for a chicken to lay Monday's, Tuesday's and Wednesday's eggs. She and the baby exchanged gazes of mutual understanding. Death looked at the mother.

"I can't have my own, "said Death, "but I would take very good care of a baby if I could have one."

The mother looked Death up and down. She'd mistaken her for a hooker but now realized she couldn't be one. Her clothes had a freshly washed, sun-dried look. Her teeth sparkled way too white. The hookers who worked these streets were table scraps. Two of her sisters were table scraps. This woman you could put in a movie. Or a painting. You could use her face to sell cigarettes, cold cream, or cola. Her face inspired.

"You can have her," whispered the mother.

Death smiled as if she'd already heard the offer.

The mother bolted, running in the direction of the cathedral. Church bells peeled and somewhere a rooster that was being made to fight his brother listened to his sibling's death rattle.

Death's skirt swished as she sang a serpentine lullaby to the baby, "Sssssssssss, sssssssssss, sssssssssssss…" She carried the little one in the direction of the paupers' cemetery. She stroked the little one's black tuft of hair. She tugged her fleshy earlobes, and she and the baby tasted the air with their tongues.

Faith, Charity, Esther, and Rose shared a room outfitted with new mattresses, pillows, and blankets. They loaded their clothes into a mahogany wardrobe and stood a gilded mirror on the mahogany desk.

Their third night in the orphanage, Faith crawled across the stone floor and curled up on the rug next to Rose's crib.

"Can I have your bed?" Esther asked Faith.

"Yes."

She pushed Faith's bed next to hers and doubled her sleep space.

On their eighth day at the orphanage, two men wheeled a dark German piano into the sisters' room. They stationed it beside the window that looked onto the rose garden.

Most of the time, the sisters stayed indoors but the matrons did herd them into the rose gardens after meals so that girls could play pretend or chase bees. After playtime on Tuesdays, an art teacher set up his easel by the crib. He set up still lives of fruits, nuts, and flowers for his students to paint. The music teacher tortured them on Fridays. A regular tutor bothered them every day except Sunday.

During playtime, Charity would tuck her easel under her arm, carry it into the courtyard, erect it near the roses, leer at their buds, and attack her canvas with watercolors. The bushes barfed especially lush and vivid blossoms where the matrons sometimes stabbed the dirt with shovels at night. They could be seen schlepping brown sacks in the moonlight, heaving these into holes, and covering them back up with loose soil. They returned in the daylight to water, trim, and weed flowerbeds.

A weekly fruit basket arrived, and the matrons would set this treat on a teacart by the girls' biggest window. They allowed the sisters to eat from it, whatever they felt like whenever they felt like it. They could eat guayaba, mango, banana, passion fruit, loquat, cherimoya, pomegranate, or mamey. The girls left their bedroom for the big meal of the day, a meal that combined lunch and dinner: linner. At linnertime, the matrons chaperoned the sisters into the high-ceilinged cafeteria with yellow and green tile floors. Long, long wood tables and benches striped the room. A matron bearing a cauldron filled with cooling pinto beans walked from sitting orphan to fidgeting orphan, scooping and slapping brown into clay bowls. Behind this broad, a woman toting a tortilla stack tossed a Frisbee at each orphan. Behind her followed a woman cradling a ewer of lukewarm water. She held its spout over each orphan's clay cup and let the water level rise till it was half full.

"Pssst," Charity called to Maria Guadalupe, the orphan sitting across from her.

"Yeah?" responded Maria Guadalupe.

"Wanna trade?" Charity gestured at her plate. Pinto beans fried in lard blew steam at Charity's chin. A hunk of bolillo the size of toddler's lower leg flexed next to them. Champurrado swelled in her terracotta mug.

"Really?" asked Maria Guadalupe.

"Yes. Your food looks better to me."

Maria Guadalupe pushed her plate at Faith while Faith pushed hers at Maria Guadalupe. Maria Guadalupe snatched the bolillo, ripped it in half, and dug her fingernails into the white, hollowing the bread till she'd turned the crust into a cone. She shoved the white into her mouth, chewed, and reached for a spoon. She scooped beans into her freshly sculpted cornucopia and took a sniff of her creation.

"Mmmm," she groaned.

"Later on," said Faith, "if you pose for me, I'll share my watermelon with you."

"Pose how?"

"So that I can paint you. You'll be my model. I'll brings my paints in here and make your picture."

"Okay."

Maria Guadalupe took a bite of beany bread. The orphan sitting next to her (also named Maria Guadalupe, almost everybody in the orphanage was named Maria Guadalupe) whispered something into her ear. Maria Guadalupe nodded. "Yes," she whispered at the girl.

Maria Guadalupe leaned towards Faith and whispered, "Tonight, we're busting out of this place."

"Why?" asked Faith. "I like it here." She picked up a boiled bean and slid it under her tongue, letting its insides ooze out of their shell.

"Yeah, well that's because you don't have to live like the rest of us."

Faith scrunched her mouth in embarrassment.

"Don't do that," said Maria Guadalupe. "I wish I had what you have. We all wish we had what you have. Anyways, tonight, we're leaving out a kitchen window. We're meeting in the courtyard with the white roses. When you hear an owl call six times, be there." She turned to the girl on her left and asked, "Are you gonna be there?" The girl nodded.

The chief Maria Guadalupe pointed at the kitchen with her spoon. "We're gonna go in there," she said. "That's where it's gonna happen."

"How are you gonna get in there?" asked Faith.

"Look under the table," said Maria Guadalupe.

Faith leaned back, bent, and stuck her head under the table. In Maria Guadalupe's lap, she saw a metal ring holding three long keys.

Charity was sitting at the desk. Candlelight illuminated the half-finished hummingbird on her needlepoint canvas. She stuck needle into wing and pulled green thread. Esther was in bed, her fingers at her eyelashes. They were busy tugging each hair individually till it popped free. Her eyelids smarted. Her green eyes stared at the ceiling. The pain warmed and distracted her. It replaced her mother.

Faith was curled on the rug next to the crib, her hand rocking it back and forth. She listened for bird sounds.

"Hoot. Hoot. Hoot. Hoot. Hoot. Hoot," came from the courtyard with yellow roses.

Faith's hand held onto the cradle slats. She continued rocking it back and forth.

I like it here, she thought to herself. *Art classes. My sisters. Interesting kids to talk to. Rose gardens outside the window. No screaming. No breaking glass. Nobody pressing their hands against my mother's mouth. Tomorrow I'll paint the sun. I'll paint him having fun.*

The next day, in the cafeteria, as the matron with the bean cauldron humped to the next table, Faith leaned towards a Maria Guadalupe sitting across from her. "Tell me about last night," she said.

Without even brokering the swap, Faith pushed her plate forward and scooted the other girl's plate closer to her chest. She picked up her spoon and dug into the watery beans.

The Maria Guadalupe said, "Well, maybe you heard it. Big Lupe hooted in the courtyard with the yellow roses, and we snuck out the windows and met her there. We tiptoed to the kitchen, and Lupe put the biggest key in the lock and turned it. We tiptoed into the kitchen and unlatched and cranked open the window by the tub. Big Lupe climbed up into it and dropped to the ground. She waited for me on the stone, and I got up onto the ledge, and I was ready to drop, but then I got scared."

"Of what?"

"Her."

"Who?" asked Faith.

A different Maria Guadalupe chimed in, "The ghost who killed her babies!"

"Oh."

The orphans were talking about their country's most famous ghost. She lives in every one of its towns, cities, villages, and imaginations, anywhere there are people who understand and misunderstand women. Sometimes she's young, sometimes she's in the middle, and sometimes she's ancient. She is, however, always a woman.

There's a version of the story that she had a family and her husband cheated on her — sometimes the cheating is with her sister, sometimes it's a best friend. To get revenge, she takes the things that are half him to the river and dunks them. She holds them down till the bubbles and the thrashing stop. *Gurgle, gurgle,* and then only *gur-.* You can only imagine the *-gle.*

In the patriotic version of the story, the drowning is merciful. Spaniards are invading Mexico and an Indian woman understands the apocalyptic nature of what's going on. So that her kids won't be raped or made into slaves, she holds their hands, walks them to a puddle — cranes and storks watch, eagles fly overhead with baby snakes in their beaks — and the Indian weeps. Her tears make a river she uses to ensure her children's freedom.

There are infinite versions of this story, you can make up your own version of this story, but the constant is that the creature who makes this story tick is a woman. A woman destroys. She creates a tiny apocalypse, the worst kind. Almost always, she uses water. Children die with moist lungs. They are held under, they thrash, they kick, they try to scream, and an axolotl, wearing a smile he can't get rid of, watches from the lake bottom. As the small body stops moving, the axolotl continues to smile. He smiled so much his face stayed that way.

"You were more scared of her than of staying in the orphanage?" asked Faith. Two Maria Guadalupes nodded so hard their faces blurred. "What did Big Lupe do?" asked Faith.

A Maria Guadalupe replied, "She took off running in the direction of the ghost. We heard hooting. We looked up, and there was an owl watching us from a nest in one of the rafters. It had yellow eyes. Its back was to us but its head was turned completely around. There was a black butterfly hovering around its shoulders. The owl craned its neck to look closer at us, and it started to look like a man, so we shut the windows fast and left the kitchen and ran back to the dormitory. We don't know what happened to Big Lupe."

"Where was she planning on going?"

Maria Guadalupe shrugged.

What do you call a reverse female orphan, the mother of a dead baby? Is she a black butterfly with a rainbow tongue? To her, does all the nectar taste sour?

When Abuelita was two weeks away from dying, my aunts and my three extra aunts came to the house for tostadas and wine from a box. Abuelito conceived these extra aunts with his mistress, and one of my regular aunts, Tía Pancha, was fine with the extra aunts being in the living room, gossiping, but Ofelia, the one who took me ice-skating in a pyramid, was not. Everybody dragged her chair and sat so that we formed a circle, and Ofelia and Mom listened to the extra aunts share stories about their father and their childhoods.

I sat in the chair that Abuelito had liked to pontificate from. I listened. I could smell Abuelita's dying process. She was dying on the other side of the house by the street but the smell carried. It crept down the hall, and it squatted with us in the room. It swirled around us, almost dancing. It was decrepit pussy with a unicorn beard, bedsores, and inertia.

I could tell from the expressions on their faces that as the extra aunts talked about growing up, Ofelia and Mom were transposing timelines of their childhoods over their half sisters' chronologies. You could tell that in their heads they were thinking stuff like, *Now I understand why my father wasn't around to wish me a happy birthday when I turned eight. Because he was at that bastard's first communion.*

Abuelita was moaning very little that night. Maybe she was straining to listen to the stories, the stories that confirmed the horror and banality of my grandfather's infidelity. As I watched the extra aunts' mouths move, I saw Abuelito talking to me. It was my first time seeing these women whose existence I'd known of for decades. For about twenty years, their existence had been a shadow in my imagination but now Abuelito's big ass nose was saluting me from their faces. His nose repeated over and over and over, and then I realized that the long shape of his face was there, too. He was haunting me through my extra aunts' faces.

The day after the three extra aunts came to eat tostadas, Ofelia took her daughter and her daughter's daughter and me downtown to buy jewelry. We strolled the jewelry district which sprawled within view of where my grandmothers had lived, the orphanage.

I announced, "I have a headache," and everyone followed me into a convenience store where I plucked a 7-Up from a refrigerator. I carried it to the counter, broke my only bill, and carried my drink outside. I slid a plastic vial of ibuprofen from my purse, popped it open, and emptied two pills onto my tongue. I washed them down. My forehead still throbbed.

To our left, near a staircase and a short palm tree, a copper man worked at a folding table. A red velvet cloth covered it and on that perched a wire cage housing a yellow bird. The bird had a job. When the man opened the cage door, the bird hopped out and onto a long box crammed with folded papers. The bird bounced along the papers till he paused. He folded his claws around one's edges. The man pinched the bird's chosen paper, bribed the animal onto his finger with birdseed, and lifted him back to his cage.

I fished money out of my jeans pocket, walked up to the table, and flashed three coins in my palm at the man.

"Can your bird tell my fortune?" I asked.

The man eyed my coins. He looked at me and said, "I'm not begging for alms."

Ofelia, her daughter, and her daughter's daughter laughed at me. I grinned to hide my embarrassment. The man turned to unfold the fortune of the woman who had been waiting with her four kids.

From under the brim of my straw hat, a straw hat whose band I sometimes tucked fortunes mined from fortune cookies, I glanced around the courtyard. I looked for Death. Maybe she was hiding behind the column supporting an office balcony. Maybe she was hiding in the ivy eating the monument bearing the city's coat of arms, a tree gripped by twin lions. Maybe she was the little yellow bird, grabbing people's fortunes from a wooden box.

On the way back to Abuelita's, I listened through my migraine as Ofelia shared with us her first memory:

She heard weeping. The sound was coming from a place without God.

Ofelia pressed her eye to the keyhole in her parents' bedroom door. She spied her mother pacing, howling, and clutching a wooden box.

The coffin carried a baby, a little boy. Abuelita hugged the box to her chest and Abuelito reached for it to take it away. Abuelita snarled and bit at him. He let her pace for days till eventually, she crumpled. Slept on the floor next to the bed where she'd given birth to death and afterbirth. When she woke up, her arms held nothing.

The Chaperones

Mrs. March was the second grown-up I came out to, and as I was psyching myself up to do so, I dangled my legs over the side of her hotel bed. She was sitting on a chair across from me. A brass table lamp lit her long head from behind. Nothing sexual was going on; Mrs. March was chaperoning twelve nerds, including me, on an overnight field trip for argumentative teens. We belonged to Junior Statesmen of America.

I'd had a feeling about my teacher that made me stand in my socks at her door and knock. I believed, in fact my heart glowed with the possibility, that I could trust her enough to tell her I'd been making out with a tomboy in eucalyptus groves behind the airport. What Mrs. March looked like had made me plant my trust in her. She had Virginia Woolf's face, Samuel Taylor Coleridge's hair, and Walt Whitman's wardrobe. What little queer wouldn't want her identity validated by a chimera like that?

After my confession, Mrs. March told me in a soothing but staunch voice, "I'm fine with you being a lesbian but I feel sad that you might never have children." Her turkey waddle jiggled as she pitied my womb, "In order to completely be, to completely be a woman, you must experience motherhood."

Since a baby hasn't grown inside me, I cannot completely be, completely be Mrs. March's kind of woman. Like a partial birth abortion, I'm partially alive. This slides me into the category of the living dead. My maternal shortcomings render me a llorona.

La llorona, Mexico's most famous ghost, is missing the same thing I am. However, at one point in her life, she would've made Mrs. March's cut for womanhood. This fabled Mexican she-creature had kids and then she fully realized herself by unhaving them. Through the unhaving, she unhad herself. In her legend which is constantly being retold, innovated, and massaged, la llorona murders her kids and then commits suicide. But isn't this just a symbolic way of expressing that obliterating motherhood obliterates womankind, that is, killing your kids is killing yourself? And yet it isn't. It isn't at all. A mother is a mother is a mother even when she isn't. Even when she never was.

La llorona is louder dead than when her lungs breathed. She's not completely gone but she's not completely here either. At night, she wanders neighborhoods, seeking replacements. She sniffs out and follows fresh baby smells to nurseries. She slips in through windows hung with alphabet curtains and lingers beside wicker bassinets. Gazing into a cradle, she thinks, *It's so beautiful. It's mine!*

Like the babies she stalks, la llorona is constantly being born. Every time a woman undoes her motherhood, a llorona is born. Some lloronas are born by arson. Conservative lloronas are born by water. Lloronas who are lazy cooks become so by microwave (yes, there are women who have microwaved their infants). My mother almost became a llorona by wooden spoon. The spoon whapped my pompis but the profound tension in my butt cheeks cracked it. Splinters rained and wood chunks stained brown by thousands of beans clattered to our kitchen linoleum. Mom and I stared at her jagged handle, now a stump she could use to dig my heart out.

Some lloronas sacrifice their eggs by loving other women. Lesbianism is the most melodramatic contraceptive.

Before I knew the word lesbian, my parents used la llorona to make me behave.

"She's looking for children," Dad would warn me, "because she drowned her own. Now she wants other people's. If she catches you wandering around the house after your bedtime, sneaking more little late-night snacks out of the fridge, she'll take you. You'll become hers. No more cartoons. You'll never see your hamster again."

The prospect of bumping into a dead lady in my dark living room made me want to toss off my sheets and grab my slippers. It made me pray to white Jesus that I would sleepwalk. Staring up at dark popcorn ceiling, I wondered, *If la llorona is powerful enough to hunt me down while I wander my house at night, what's to stop her from crawling into my bed and reaching her arms around me?* My cheek pressed to nosebleed-stained pillow. My toes waited for her tickle. I worked myself into a hallucinatory state where I believed the air space around my body was alive, electric with her haunting.

Since la llorona is a spirit, she leaves her passport on her nightstand when she travels. She wafts north into the United States to midwife her rebirth as an American. A Yanqui.

Shaquan Duley — a South Carolina woman who looks in her mugshot how I imagine Precious, the shero of Sapphire's masterpiece, *Push*, might look — recreated herself as a llorona. She placed her hands over her toddlers' mouths till their breaths dried up. Afterwards, she strapped their bodies into car seats and waited on the riverbank. She watched her Chrysler roll into the Edisto. It sank into the black water as she walked away.

Shaquan sat for an interview with Oprah. The piece was titled THE MOM WHO KILLED HER SONS. In the interview, prison bars glow behind Shaquan and Oprah. Oprah repeats, "How were you able to do that?" Repeated, the question turns into a chant. The chant implies accusation. Shaquan weeps instead of answering. Oprah changes her question to "Whom did you suffocate first?"

As Shaquan replies, Oprah condemns her with her eyes. Shaquan describes killing her kids as an out-of-body experience. She doesn't say this but, maybe, since she can leave her body, maybe sometimes Shaquan's soul floats through the bars, past the prison watchtowers. It (souls don't have a gender) touches down at the river. It moans, "Where are my children? Where are my babies…?"

When Shaquan killed her kids, a lot of people drew comparisons to another llorona, a white one, Susan Smith. I was seventeen when Susan, also of South Carolina, was cheating on her husband. Susan's lover told her that her least sexy characteristic was motherhood. To become sexier, Susan strapped her kids into their car seats and watched her Mazda roll into John D. Long Lake.

Susan exercised less mercy than Shaquan. She rolled her sons to their deaths while they breathed. Their small nostrils inhaled lake. Their lungs became water balloons. Tadpoles swam into their ear canals.

While my family ate, we listened to the TV. We listened to Susan twang, "It hurts to know that, um, that I would be accused, or thought that I would ever do anything to harm my children." This ineloquent sound bite repeated as Susan's false story of a black man driving off with her kids during a carjacking looped on the news. The day after All Souls Day, Susan confessed. Divers swam to her car and found her children floating upside down.

I was sitting in my Catholic high school's gym, yawning through the annual Mothers' Mass when, from the altar erected below a basketball hoop, Father Stephen urged, "...remember to pray for all mothers, including Susan Smith." As he continued his sermon, I glanced around. My gaze bumped into mothers glancing around, too. They were making rotten cheese faces, like, *Did that faggot just say what I think he said?*

My blood felt warm and fuzzy. Hotly carbonated. I formed fists and smiled. I was pleased the priest had upset so many women of leisure by bringing up a llorona, especially one with the same color as them.

Time magazine put Susan on a cover. They chose a picture of her where she looks like a saint with downcast eyes, a Marian apparition. The words "How Could She Do It?" scrolled down the right side of her face. I never told my friends, my mom, Mrs. March, or the tomboy I was making out with, but *Time's* question baffled me. A mother killing her kids seemed like the most natural thing in the world to me. I came to this conclusion through make-believe, through a childhood game called Push. A game where one person flails on a mattress, faking labor, while another person stands between their legs yelling, "PUSH!"

The person pushing always has more fun. It's the most fun if you push so hard you die, and your playmate has to drag you by your feet to the yard to bury you. Even as a kid playing Push, I understood that the things you love most are the things that wind up killing you, so why not beat them to it?

Andrea Yates is another white llorona. Looking at her mugshot doesn't evoke any literary protagonists. However, her stare. It's clear that insanity anchors her stare. Andrea and her husband practiced hardcore Christianity in a hardcore place, Texas. He kept her belly swollen despite warning signs that birth control might have prevented her from becoming what she was bound to become. Having babies made her hands tremble. By the time she had her fourth, Andrea was whispering, "Help." Demonic voices spoke inside her head. Listen. Can you hear them, too? Can you hear pretend babies being born?

Andrea came to believe Satan had wormed inside her. He lived in her blood and marrow. She believed she'd messed up her kids to the point that they couldn't be fixed. She decided to use her bathtub to purify them. In order of age, she held them underwater. After dunking each one, she placed them on her bed and pulled a sheet over them.

Her oldest, Noah, screamed, "I know what you're doing!" and ran away from her.
She chased him around the house, caught up to him, grabbed him, dragged him back to the bathroom, and made broth with him.

Andrea was sentenced to a mental hospital instead of prison. Now, she sits at a table. She sews aprons that customers buy and wear to keep their clothes clean while they're tossing carrots into crockpots.

Lloronas are still being made in Mexico. Last year, in Guanajuato, a state famous for its accidental mummies, a woman whom Mexican newscasters described as "desnaturalizada," unnatural, decided to unhave her children. She was working at a shoe factory. Instead of smashing her kids with chanclas, a Mexican's preferred weapon against cockroaches, she drowned them. To get rid of what was left, she drove their bodies to the countryside. After piling them on the dirt, she struck a match and let it fall. Pumpkin flames consumed the bodies till their meat was charred. Grilled bones and buttons remained.

When reporters asked why she did what she did, the shoemaker replied, "Somebody had to die. And it was them."

Reporters asked her, "Why didn't you kill yourself?"

"I tried," she answered. "But I failed."

An uploaded video about her crimes is titled SHE DROWNS AND BURNS HER CHILDREN.

SHE drowns SHE burns HER children

Men lifted the skeletons, loaded them onto gurneys, and carried them to vans.

Am I related to the shoemaker? Maybe. Abuelita gave birth to Mom in a house in Jalisco. Jalisco bordered the shoemaker's pyre.

In March, Ebony Wilkerson drove her Honda into the Daytona Beach surf. Onlookers and a lifeguard made tracks across the sand, chasing the minivan into waves. One caught up with Ebony, who was behind the wheel as if possessed. From the backseat, a child screamed, "Please help us! Our mom is trying to kill us!" The men rescued the children and Ebony was sent to a hospital.

Two months after trying to wash her kids to death, Ebony welcomed her fourth child.

During the birth, the Cihuateteo whispered, "Push," into Ebony's ear.

The Cihuateteo are the ageless ghosts of women who've died during childbirth. It's been thousands of years and they still haven't forgiven the babies that tore them to death. Those brats stole from them the ability to be. They are just like this sentence (incomplete)

According to the Aztec ritual calendar, the Cihauateteo share our dirty planet. Like Mrs. March, they chaperone the sun to hell every night but make sure it returns to the sky each morn. When the Cihauateteo aren't hanging out with our solar system's light source, they roam kitchens, porches, lakeshores, beaches, driveways, and shoe factories. They hold hands with children. No one living can be sure of what the Cihuateteo do with the kids that they take for long walks. Statues of the Cihuateteo show them bearing clawed feet, flashing dry, broken nipples. They rustle, wearing skirts made of husks.

Her face is an open-mouthed skull. Her teeth are ready. Her teeth say everything completely and incompletely.

SPOILER ALERT: If You Haven't Read Toni Morrison's Pulitzer Prize-Winning Novel But Plan To, Skip Ahead

Dad looked up from a glossy tabloid he was faggily reading. He said, "Michelle Obama is no Jackie O. Jackie O was pretty. Michelle Obama looks like Mohammad Ali."

Lifting the magazine, Dad turned it to show me Mrs. Obama. If all Dad was going by was *that* particular picture, a candid photo that vastly overemphasized the First Lady's jawline, he was right. However, I responded by saying, "You're a racist."

Of all the names you can call an American, "racist" is the worst. The accusation flusters. You get to watch them say interesting things in self-defense. Dad was ignoring me.

"You're racist," I repeated. He kept reading about the Obamas. I ordered, "Name a pretty black woman."

Dad answered calmly and succinctly, as if he'd been anticipating this prompt, "The ghost from that movie *Beloved*."

"Thandie Newton?"

"Yes. The ghost from *Beloved* is pretty. Very pretty. Beautiful. She looks like your mommy."

"Anybody else? What about Oprah?"

Dad repeated, "I like the ghost from *Beloved*."

"Mo-om!" I yelled. Mom was standing at the kitchen sink, rinsing a head, a head of iceberg lettuce, lechuga. "Dad thinks the ghost from *Beloved* is pretty!" I tattled.

Mom looked at us across the tiled counter, shrugged her shoulders, blew a playful cobweb of white hair off her cheek, and declared, "Yo soy mas bonita!"

MY MOTHER THINKS SHE'S PRETTIER THAN THE GHOST OF A FICTIONAL SLAVE BABY CRUSHED TO DEATH BY HER OWN MOTHER IN A MANNER REMINISCENT OF THE LEGENDARY LLORONA.

Is that saying much? Yes.

Thandiwe Nashita Newton, the British actress who played a dead slave child returning to haunt her surviving family as an insatiable ghost in Oprah's film adaptation of Toni Morrison's *Beloved* is, physically, a goddess. While I have been known to envy my mother's beauty, more than that I envy her ability to assert such irreverent self-esteem.

Chaparral

Dirt slopes sandwiched the mesa our long white house sprawled along. If you picture the property like a moon pie in three layers, then the cream is one story's worth of three-car garage, half bathroom, pantry, laundry room, dining room, breakfast nook, living room, family room, fireplace, foyer, hallways, master bedroom, master bathroom, kids' rooms, and kids' bathroom surrounded by lawn and patio and veranda and arbors and a shed and plants. Our four-bedroom house looked traditional. Not Paul Revere traditional, California traditional. A red brick porch that smelled good after rain, and red bricking around the living room and dining room windows.

I chose green for our shutters, and cleaned and painted them. Ixchel's room looked onto dreary rabbit hutches by some crab apple trees that the house's previous owners had abandoned. Dad's axe hacked these to shipwrecks, and he and I wore matching gloves while we stuffed their remains into trashcans. Those cans sometimes held living things. Driving country roads, we might see a big rope sunning itself on the asphalt. Antonio would squeal, "Daddy, a king snake!" and Dad would pull our minivan to the shoulder, get out, creep along the pavement, grab a snake by her tail, and drop her into an empty firewood box that happened to be in the corner.

Antonio, Ixchel, and I rode staring at the snake box. Dad's sweatshirt covered it. We pulled into our neighborhood which had no sidewalks in order to make it feel extra country. We drove up our driveway that we weren't allowed to ride our bikes down anymore. One time, I talked Ixchel into riding hers down it. She zoomed, struck a pebble, caught air, and became E.T. silhouetted against the moon. A eucalyptus tree stopped her and turned her nose into a latke for a couple of months.

Parking on the driveway's level slab beside the loquat tree, Dad prepared. He hurried to the green trashcan and heaved garbage out of it, setting its sacks near our gas meter. He scampered back to the van, picked up the firewood box, and walked it to the can. He shook off the sweatshirt, and gently emptied the snake into the trashcan. I tiptoed to the can and leaned over it. Snake coiled at the bottom where stink and grime, *mugre* in Spanish (what a delicious word), lived in the creases and ruts. The snake didn't like it down there. You could tell she was going to make herself anorexic or something. Not eat. We could release Hamlin's rats in there and she'd let them crawl all over her, use her as a futon. She would shrink pipe cleaner thin.

After a week of enjoying a snake in our trashcan, we put her back in the box and drove her back into the hinterlands, beyond camel-colored mountains whose names I didn't know. We traveled beyond the dump, the wineries, the vineyards, and the Satanic Church. The Satanic Church wasn't really a satanic church. It was a lone whitewashed Victorian chapel led to by rows of poplar. No one worshiped there. It was abandoned so everyone said Satanists worshipped there. It did look like an ideal place for child sacrifice. It was a landmark. One of those fake-dangerous landmarks every place has. A good place for losing your virginity.

At the creek, we parked. Sycamores shaded the minivan. Dad opened its sliding door. My foot pushed the box. Its mouth plunged forward. With a stick, Dad wrangled the snake out. She squirmed, plopped to the dirt, and slithered into poison oak. Rustle. Wildcats stopped to listen. Acorns sat silently. Chumash Indian ghosts quit being recluses. They emerged from the chaparral and put their ears to the homecoming.

"Welcome, sssssssssssssnake…" I imagined them saying. The women were topless. Ghost tits absorbed the afternoon sunlight.

I saved a snake's life once. Mom had taken out the trash. I realized a snake we'd caught and dumped in a can must've been gasping under the weight of her mistake. I left the TV, sprinted down the front porch and past Mom's diseased roses, and hoisted out the sack. I set it next to the gas meter. The snake hissed, "Thank you, human…"

Two-thirds of our property we called "the hill." A third had no name. This part was the housey part surrounded by the patio and lawn and stuff.

On our lawn, Dad raged against gophers. They fucked with him like furry Viet Cong. They fucked with us, too. Playing soccer in the front yard, your ankle plunged and twisted down a hole. Mom's rhododendrons browned. Gophers were nibbling things roots first. Mounds bumped the grass. Dirt measles.

On his garage worktable, Dad stockpiled traps, bait, and poison. The bait looked like trail mix. I was a hippo. Eat it? I considered it.

I followed Dad to a hole. I studied him as he knelt to set traps. Squatting so that he got fatherly camel toe, Dad pulled back metal pieces and eased a contraption down into a gopher lair but not too deep. His stubby fingers lifted poison and bait sacks. Trail mix and death sprinkled into the black hole. What would happen if I rolled a golf ball inside? A white string tied Dad's trap to a six-inch wood stake he stabbed it into the grass. He could've been Van Helsing. He had a beard and Slavic eyes. Dad was half Polish. Close enough. Close enough to Transylvanian.

Everyday, standing beside the brick column supporting the porch overhang, Dad watched his stakes. He was checking: were they up or crooked?

Finally, one was twitching.

"We got one!" Dad sprinted to the stake. He pulled it out of California and pulled the trap from the hole. The gopher was squirming. His claws scratched at the air. He was a rhododendron fat ass. Metal clamped his neck but he struggled to churn his head. He raged. Dad smacked his Viet Cong against the grass. It was like slapping a gopher with a pillow. Too fun. Dad needed something to really euthanize him. We speed walked across the lawn, past the garage doors to the trashcans. Rainwater filled the chocolaty one. Dad dunked the gopher into the deep and held the stake a foot above the liquid. How deep the gopher went, I don't know. Gopher bubbles popped along the surface. Rodent raged against the dying of the light. Sloshing, the rainwater grew carbonated, then flattened. Dad pulled the string up. Tunnel rat sleek, plump, dead. Defeated. Water dripped from claws. Awesome.

Lawn was necessary evil. It looked suburban and cushioned spills. You could play croquet or Indians scalping settlers there.

Maybe lawn mowing turned me gay. Since I was the eldest, Dad handed me the mower. I pushed it forward and right, forward and right, losing some hearing, losing my heterosexuality as grass bled onto my sneakers. My calves, hips, and ass grew toned. I shed blubber. I shed any attraction I had to boys. Jelly stained my underwear. I mowed the lawn with cramps. I weedwacked hard-to-reach tufts. I wielded the leaf blower, pointed it at tree skirts. Have you even seen a twelve-year-old girl with a leaf blower? It's butch. The lawn mower is *la podadora* in Spanish. The blower is *el blower*. Mom taught me that. She disliked el blower. She told me, "It's a shortcut." She hid it from me and forced me to sweep the back patio with a push broom. Sweep around her barrel cacti. Her wisteria made a delicate mess.

The hill intimidated. You got a sense that ancient tragedy lived there. Dad's most terrifying threat? "Keep it up and you'll have to weed the hill."

Sisyphus laughed.

Front hill, back hill, one hill. We moved into the hill house when I was ten and Dad had plans for plants. The people who'd owned the house before us had their lawns, rabbits, crab apple trees, rosebushes, and foreigners living on the hill. Foreigners included pampas grasses from South America and cape daisy from Africa. Bushwhacked birds of paradise. Gross. These uglies encouraged erosion. Their idiot roots made the hill spit and crumble. Mini-avalanches rolled past the backyard retaining wall, shitting onto backyard lawn. Out front, more dirt slid into the street. It turned mud. Dirt that Dad had paid more than a hundred thousands dollars for washed down asphalt and into gutters. It poured down sewers. It emptied into the Pacific Ocean. It wedded sea floor.

California native plants know how to keep California from disintegrating. They have the roots to hold our shit firm. Dad bought books about this native power and took us on excursions to see native plant power at Santa Barbara's botanical gardens. We hit the native plant nursery circuit, too. Dad was also open to stuff that grew well in Mediterranean climates. Things that flex their muscles in places like Turkey or Greece. Because of my upper body strength, Dad elected me his botanical wingman.

Driving along the 101 freeway, which is deadly picturesque, I looked at herbaceous clumps clouding barbed wire fences. Blonde cows chewing. "That," Dad said, "is Coyote Brush. It's an ingredient in our local chaparral. Deer hate it."

"What's chaparral?"

"That bushy layer you see everywhere."

Learning the names of my state's native plants vibrated my spirit.

"Ah, see the forest on those hills?" Dad asked. The foliage looked blackish. Mossy canopies shaded crevices where hills rubbed together. Trunks curved, hot women and crones. Hot crones. Barky crones. Branches cast twig reels, fishing. Foothills existed for oaken conquest.

"Yes."

"They're Quercus agrifolia. Coast Live Oak. We're going to get some for the hill."

I pictured myself bent and scooping acorns off the hill. I held up my suede loincloth's flap. I dropped nuts into it till it was full. My bare feet carried me to potholes carved into a boulder. I emptied my pile into a hole and picked up a rock. Pounded my acorns. My efforts made meal. Spreading it across the rock, I looked up. Felt droplets. Rain was washing my cheeks. Rain purged acorn tannins and washed my flat chest. Tannin is poison. *Ghghgghghghghg,* I hocked a loogie onto my meal. It congealed, turning doughy, and I plopped onto my nalgas. I kneaded tortillas and johnnycakes on the stone. I dangled them over oak twig campfires I willed into existence with my mind. The possum bone in my septum reflected the flames. My fantasy hybridized Aztec and Chumash, acorn and human sacrifice. I disposed of my acorn trash in the midden. Archeologists would find my refuse and piece together my identity. Acorn Aztec. Acorn bitch of the hill.

"See that?" Dad pointed at a flowering plant creeping along roadside. It was a gourd patch without fruit. Large white flowers, fluted Victrolas.

"Yes?"

"Don't ever touch that. It's poison. Every piece of it. Somebody should get rid of it."

"What is it called?"

"Jimson weed."

"What happens if you eat it?"

"If you're lucky, you'll see God and only get a little brain damage."

"What else?"

"You vomit. You shake. You stop breathing. You have seizures. Die. Same thing that happens if you feed me banana." I already knew the dangers of feeding Dad bananas. He kept his distance from the lunchtime fruit. He also warned us that if we picked at the moles that looked like kernels of hamburger meat clinging to his neck, he'd bleed to death. I wanted to at least try.

We hoofed muddy nursery aisles. Dad pointed at rows. "Sugar bush." "Coffee berry." "Lemonade berry." My stomach growled. I loaded the smallish things on our shopping list into a smallish wagon I pulled behind me. Dad loaded the biggish things into his bigger dolly. We dragged our carts over dark dirt to this hut-type thing. Dad handed a hippie cashier a check, and then said, "To the Batmobile, Robin!"

Gravel crunched under my velcro shoes. Gravel felt a rain of leaves and flower buds that chafed against my sweatpants. Buckwheats. Ceanothus. Flannelbush. Wild grape. Monkey flower. Opuntias. Firs. Baccharis. Quercus agrifolia. Dad left our backseat in the garage so that we could pack the minivan floor. My hands ferried black plastic containers to him. I passed him fragile Howard McMinn manzanitas. I ogled the California jungle we filled the backseat with. Dad slid the door shut. We hopped back in, pilot and wingman. We headed back to the hill, two native sons.

We pulled shit out of the hill. Eviction time, bitches. Hoes, pickaxes, and shovels callused our palms and fingers. We dug foul roots from our soil and sent foreigners to the guillotine. Machete. We dumped stupid plants in the trash. There weren't any snakes in there.

Dad and I planted our natives on the hill. I loved them but they looked disappointing. The natives in the canyons looked mature and permanent. They were ethereal. They knew Chumash Adam and Eve. These natives acted shy. They were contemporaries of call waiting. Some didn't like their new home and committed suicide. Most remained. Where something failed, Dad substituted. He'd find something that worked with the soil. He'd flip through his native plant guides and talk to the men at the nurseries — it was all men — hippie men sold plants, trafficked in chlorophyll, and Dad experimented until he found the right native. Dad had vision. His brain performed time-lapse photography to age the hill. He saw the beauty it would be twenty years in the future. I had no vision. I hated the hill's underdeveloped look. The hill didn't even need a training bra. Its oaks weren't women. They weren't ready to swim in the deep end. They were barely climbing out of the baby pool.

I grew bitchy towards plants. I just wanted to hang out at the country club and flirt with the lifeguard. It made me feel proud when he looked at me. His eyeballs felt the short climb was worth it. My feet gripped the sunbaked edge stenciled with the words 8 FEET. The lifeguard strutted past. Red shorts went *swish, swish, swish.* I didn't see his hands but I felt them. My balance fled and I plunged. Opening my eyes, I saw kids from their necks down, dog paddling, and my limbs scrambled to break through the surface.

"*Pwwwwwwwha,*" I exhaled. My fingers reached for the edge. I was gasping, climbing out of the blue like a girl in a music video, my hair slicked back, my t-shirt dripping. Water dripped from the tip of my nose. My eyebrow hairs dripped. I shivered beside the white diving board. The lifeguard watched from his high chair. Junipers shaded him. He wore sunglasses. His legs hung open like a ghost was giving him a lap dance.

Antonio and Ixchel tattled to Dad how the lifeguard had shoved me into the deep end. Dad called the country club president. She waddled from her end of the block to ours. In her brown muumuu, the big gray-haired lady stood at the bottom of the hill. I was pushing the broom. Sweeping the driveway was my punishment for coming home wet. I was working in stretch pants. At least I looked presentable in them now, no longer like a baked potato.

Dad was standing beside me. He was wearing gardening gloves caked in California. His beard bristled.

"Tell her," he commanded.

"I was standing by the diving board," I told the president. "I was watching my brother and sister swim. Then the lifeguard came up from behind. I think he was just tickling me but I lost my balance and fell into the water."

"Okay," she said. "That's all I needed to know."

The president turned. She waddled back up our street. Dad headed towards his newly planted avocados. The hill and I watched the woman. We both knew the lifeguard was about to get a phone call. The president would tell him, "You're not a lifeguard anymore. But it's not like you ever were."

Antonio was chasing a toad across the grass. I was supervising. Something was humming. It seemed like it was coming from the hill. We weren't supposed to walk there. It had a fancy drip irrigation system. Thin plastic tubes lined its soil, feeding water crumbs. "No playing on the hill." Dad knew our feet would tear up his tubing. We'd be clumsy, puppies playing with Ming vases, and he'd have to put everything back together which would be painstaking, like using a starved mosquito as a voodoo doll.

Yes, the humming was coming from the hill. Fuck the drip; I tiptoed from grass to dirt. I tiptoed past immature coffee berry to where the sound was coming from. Wings clouded air. From the stick branch of a Quercus agrifolia hung a beehive. It was khaki and dainty. A sack lunch full of honey.

"Antonio!" I called. "Come here!" He appeared at the lawn's edge. His glasses were two lenses of pure sun. "Come here!"

"What is it?" he asked.

"Bees."

I hiked back to the lawn.

We went inside and found Mom.

"There are bees on the hill," we told her.

She told Dad. He opened the phone book on our kitchen counter and flipped through the yellow pages. He grabbed the phone receiver off the kitchen wall, pushed buttons, and spoke. Very professionally, Dad introduced himself and got to it. "Do you handle bees?" Laughter roared. I didn't know how the bee person answered but Dad arranged an appointment.

The next afternoon, the beekeeper came. He drove a white van uphill, parked, and the white man emerged. He looked like a beekeeper. He walked towards us, stork-legged and wearing a chambray shirt and gray work pants. His hair had been white for a long time. He wore a pith helmet. The kind of hat that you wear when you kill a rhinoceros. It charmed me. When was the last time we'd had an old white man in a pith helmet on our property? Never. He strode like an herbivore who enjoyed top floor leaves. He was going to take our bees. Mom and Dad made small talk about how dangerous it was to mix kids and bees. Pith helmet nodded. As a clump, the six of us traveled down the driveway. At the street, we continued along where the sidewalk should've been. After the mailbox and some lupines, Dad pointed at the oak.

"So this is what the buzz is all about?" asked the beekeeper.

Dad chuckled. "Yup," he answered.

The beekeeper became God. His hiking boots stepped into dirt. He strode past coyote brush, Manzanita, and monkey flower. He arrived at the oak. With his face, ears, neck, and hands exposed, he grabbed the hive. He tore it from its branch and whipped open a green sack. The sack ate the hive. A few stragglers made constellations, polka-dotted his shirt, then disappeared.

We were riding country roads. Gardeners drove past in their pick up, accordion music blaring out their windows.

"If I had a gardening business," said Dad, "I'd call it 'The Marquis de Sod.'"

We got home from running errands. All of us were carrying grocery bags. I saw something on the porch. I set my bag down on the cement and ran to it. I knelt before the brick. Two jars gleamed in Saturday afternoon light. They half-sat on a small note that read, "Your honey."

Lawns spread from bay windows to curbs. Palms towered beside wrought iron mailboxes. English gardens colonized little chunks of

California. Our neighbors recreated London. They could afford the water bill. Conspicuous consumption through landscaping. Look at my roses. Behold, my foxglove.

It was Sunday. I went outside to mow. The hill seemed funny. I walked down the driveway to the street to check it out. I stood in the middle of the lane. Toilet paper blanketed the hill. It looked dumb. In a traditional American yard, with its lawn, lawn jockeys, elms, daises, and asters, toilet paper reads as disrespect. On our natives, it hardly read. Oh, look, it snowed, maybe. Summer gloom wetted and was melting the TP. It was composting right in front of my eyes.

While I pushed the lawn mower, Dad, red-faced, crouched in the dirt, checking his drip irrigation. I know he wanted to do to the toilet-paperers what he did to the gophers.

The toilet paperers had used sugar to spell the word BITCH down our driveway. Guess whose job it was to sweep BITCH into the street. Sugar BITCH.

I was wearing tight black pants and a black shirt and was flopped on my bed, reading *Queen of the Damned*. Screaming interrupted the story. I sprang to my window, pulled my yellowing drape and looked. Nobody was on my lawn. Was the screaming coming from the hill? Was the sound coming from an effigy mound? No, the wail was Ixchel's. I ran outside and across the lawn and peered over the edge of the hill.

By cedars guarding the house where the one-eyed widow lived, some shithead was pinning Ixchel's arms behind her back. She screamed, but not actual words. In the middle of the street, three bullies were crowding around Antonio. The blondest one, the dentist's son, punched his fist into my brother's stomach. Antonio founded his school's chess club. He had to wear goggles to play soccer because his retinas were barely attached. People like him can only be hit with feathers. I saw red. I am a Taurus.

Boys and Ixchel watched me emerge from the hill. Bitch born of hill.

"Let my brother go!" I boomed and stepped into the street.

The dentist's son laughed. His fist rammed into Antonio's chest again.

My skin could feel the heat coming off the dentist's son. My body was in flight. My feet were off the ground and my black wings were spreading. They were expansive. A California condor's. Boys watched with their mouths open. My wings turned back into hands and reached for the dentist's son's neck. They gripped as though his neck was a Louisville Slugger. Fingers squeezed and I swung the dentist's son in a circle. He rode the bitch carousel. The one-eyed widow's cedars and the white barn at the end of the road and the optometrist's house with the palm tree and boring hedges, a zoetrope telling landscape stories over and over and over. I watched the dentist's son's face redden. Purple. Blue. I wanted him to match the sky and then I wanted to watch him rot. Turn into broccoli.

Ixchel's fear migrated to the boys. "Let him go!" they yelled. I didn't want to. The hill was giving me power. A strange noise formed in the dentist's son's throat. It was a stifled death rattle. I quit spinning. My hands unclenched. A frozen bitch, I watched my victim blink and twitch. White people color returned to his face. He was breathing again, high on some hormone, and he began to swim away. His crew jogged after him. They ran up the street, towards where the road curved left. At the turn, the dentist's son stopped. He stood near ivy, panting.

"I'm coming back!" he threatened.

"I look forward to strangling you again!" I shouted back. The hill wanted his blood.

The dad of the boy I strangled went crazy. My best friend told me so. She said all he did was stare out his bedroom window at the vineyard that swelled behind his across-the-street neighbor's house. He wore his bathrobe non-stop. He cackled so big you could see his fillings. Maybe he filled himself. He was a dentist. My best friend knew he went crazy because her mom heard from a doctor's wife who worked in the same medical building as him. I wondered if he'd kill himself. In my public speaking class, a girl did an informative speech about her dad killing himself. He'd been a dentist, then he gassed himself. I wondered if the ivy that covered the dentist's yard had anything to do with his madness. Ivy is a crazy plant. Sometimes, I thought I saw the dentist. I thought I saw someone unshaven in a brown robe at his balcony's French doors.

The dentist recovered from his madness, and one afternoon, he and his wife were driving their BMW down country roads. They saw a car accident at a hill by broccoli fields. Ooh, it was ugly, and since the dentist was a doctor, he pulled over to help. He walked to the smashed up car and found his youngest son crushed in the passenger seat. The kid behind the wheel, who was not crushed at all, was the only Jewish kid in our neighborhood. The dentist carried his son from the wreck and placed his body near an irrigation ditch. According to my best friend, a light wind blew as the bully's soul left. I felt bad for the Jewish kid. First, you're the only Jewish kid in the neighborhood. Then your shitty driving kills the crazy dentist's son.

There's a picture of me I can't find. It's from the summer before I went to college. In it, I'm at the Santa Barbara Botanic Garden, by their redwoods. Dad shot the image with his 35-millimeter camera from the top of some stone stairs. I'm looking up at him, my eyes green with forest. I'd asked to go to the gardens. He'd taken me. It'd been so long since plants had dwarfed me, and I'd been happy about it.

Chihuawhite

I got obsessed with a moth, a Mexican Goth. She wore black bodysuits. When she stomped, her saddlebags jiggled. Her lazy eye took long siestas. Talked in its sleep. Her good eye was robust. Enlightened. I always saw it reading.

After spying on the moth for weeks, I came to believe that Satan had handcrafted her for me. She was la walking dead uglier than Frida Kahlo, probably hecha en México para esta budding lesbianita. I wondered if she tasted like cilantro.

The moth managed the second floor mall bookstore. Everyone who worked at that bookstore was hot. Everyone who worked at the first floor mall bookstore was white and ugly.

To get close to the moth, I volunteered across the street at the library. The librarian put me to work paging books, which is a fancy way of saying I shelved. I washed books, too. People say money is the filthiest thing handled by humans but the boogers, minestrone, and cum I massaged with a rag off Curious George taught me that it'd be more hygienic to pleasure a thousand pennies than to kiss a single library card.

I took breaks to go spy on the moth. I skulked through the bookstore entrance and lurked in Magazines. I lurked in Science Fiction. I crouched amidst Art and Photography coffee table books. My asymmetrical eyes peeked across the top shelf of Do-It-Yourself.

Stalking excited me. I brushed my hair for it. I applied lipstick. I polished my combat boots. I tore extra holes in my dress. I bleached my facial hair.

I got the balls to walk up to the register and say, "Hi, I always see you reading. Wow. Good for you. Who are your favorite writers?"

In a baby voice that contradicted her sinister look, the moth recited a list until closing time, "Sylvia Plath, Anton Chekov, Carson McCullers, Anne Sexton, Octavio Paz, Martín Espada, Charlotte Perkins Gilman, Kate

Chopin, Shel Silverstein."

(Shel Silverstein???)

"Dostoyevsky, Tolstoy, Sophocles, all the people who wrote the Holy Bible, Anne Rice, Stephen King, Nietzsche, H.P. Lovecraft..."

With my allowance, I bought some books by the authors she mentioned. I stole the rest from the library. I slept with them under my bed. I absorbed their influence through nocturnal osmosis.

I lurked with such tenacity I earned the moth's trust.

She said, "Come to my house."

I said, "Okay."

We rode the city bus. In her parents' almost bare living room, the moth introduced me to her mother.

"Mucho gusto," I said to her.

The moth's mother mutely grinned. Her silver teeth glowed. A white lightning bolt streaked her hair's center part. Lumpy tits rode at her elastic waistband. I respected her.

In the moth's cocoon — that's a moth's bedroom — I knelt on the black and white checked floor. For a bed, the moth had what appeared to be a homemade coffin. A child-size crucifix served as its headboard.

"Can I get in?" I asked, pointing.

The moth turned her stereo louder. "Go ahead."

I climbed into her tomb. I folded my arms in an X across my chest. I closed my eyes. I was practicing.

A few weeks later at the mall pizza place I lunched with the moth, telling her about a new athletic record I'd set in PE: a thirty-minute mile.

She laughed. She laughed so hard, she farted. It sounded like a tiny pebble shot out from between her nalgas. I wondered if it was trapped in her calzones.

"You remind me of me!" cried the moth.

"Did you have a long mile, too?" I asked.

"I never ran the mile."

"Did you forge a doctor's excuse?"

"No, I refused to run it. I had conscientious objector status."

"You conscientiously rejected physical education?"

"Yes."

I wanted to impress the moth so badly that I blurted, "A boy I know got expelled for coming to school dressed as Courtney Love!"

She countered, "Before dropping out, I almost got expelled for a costume, too."

Of course she did. "What'd you go dressed as?" I asked.

She grinned and explained, "My best friend, Veronica, and I borrowed sneakers, thick socks, acid-washed jean skirts, and pink t-shirts. We put our hair up in scrunchies and got orange cover-up and smeared it on so that you could see the gross change in color between our necks and our faces. We said 'like' a lot." Her lazy eye stirred.

"You went to school dressed as white girls?"

She nodded.

The moth moved out of her parents' house near Fremont Park to her boyfriend's apartment, also near Fremont Park. One weekend when the boyfriend went to see the Grateful Dead, the moth had me over to smoke hashish. On her davenport, we sucked a joint down to a roach. My eyes felt loose.

"Once, when I was little…" the moth was saying, speaking to me from inside an intergalactic prism, "in Chihuahua, I got up in the middle of the night to go to the bathroom. I was walking and at the end of the hall I saw a woman in a white nightgown. She said, 'Come here,' and held out her arms. I walked over to her. When I put my arms around her, I fell. I felt for her but there was no one there."

"I felt things, too, when I was little," I offered quietly.

Ignoring my admission of childhood clairvoyance, the moth continued, "One time, when she was about thirteen, my mom was at her friend's house. They were sleeping in different beds, and my mom woke up in the middle of the night with a shadow on top of her. It was crushing her." I had a vision of a Rorschach inkblot dry-humping the moth except the moth had her mother's hair. "She tried screaming but she couldn't move. She was paralyzed." The moth paused. "The shadow disintegrated and my mom was just, like, there. Awake all night. Like a week later, my mom's friend said to her, 'Patricia, remember that night you slept over? Something happened. Something got on top of me and...' "

I visualized two ectoplasmic rapists laughing at the border fence.

It turned out that the moth was keeping a secret. Her Halloween prank, her whiteface, had invited a white spirit into her body. The white demon took full possession of her and not even the best local curandera, a witch doctor named Elvira, could exorcise the whiteness with a limpia. A limpia involves a white (not racially) witch waving or rubbing an egg across the sufferer's body. The egg sucks out the bad, and then the witch breaks the egg. She empties the contents into a bowl. The witch will say, "Look."

She will point at a red fleck dotting the yolk. What was your affliction may now be turned into breakfast, but scoop out that freckle first.

The demon made the moth break up with her hippie boyfriend and hop a boxcar. She rode across Oregon state lines and hopped off where it smelled the greenest and wettest. The moth changed her gorgeous Mexican name, Guadalupe Jesús de Guadalupe, to Dylan. She joined the Daughters of the American Revolution. She seduced a ginger lumberjack. He knocked her up. They named their twin daughters Ary and An.

Dylan, the lumberjack, and their twins live just outside of Eugene, in a handmade log cabin surrounded by spruces and hard-working beavers. Dylan manages a faux taxidermy shop/vegan cupcakery. She shows her work — billions of handcrafted paper napkin snowflakes — at the local art gallery. She counts nettle, kelp, and imitation venison among her favorite flavors. She composts everything, including her past. The only word ghosts whisper to her now is in English: Boo.

An omen slunk to the middle of the road. A frosty milk carton rode in a paper bag on our backseat. Maybe the black cat had sensed the dairy and been attracted by it. Black cats like lapping Vitamin D from dishes set by backdoors. They grab mice by their tails and dangle them over chilled cups of cream.

The omen stiffened on a white dash mark. Her fur flattened. Her chin tilted down. Her whiskers got a hard on. Yellow eyes stared at our incoming bumper, challenging us.

"Speed bump!" Dad announced.

My fingers gripped my armrest. A dragonfly exploded against the windshield. Gutsy.

That we were about to kill something dark and agile stole my breath. We flew right over her, roaring over her heartbeat, and I turned. My seatbelt wrestled me, and I twisted and lunged against yanks and snaps.

Looking over my shoulder, I gazed across the backseat out the dusty rear window. In one sleek piece, the black cat was sitting in golden roadside grass. A grasshopper arced into the air beside her, landing in our lane.

"Did I get it?" asked Dad.

"No."

Dad absorbed the disappointment. Then he lectured, "Never brake for animals. If you're ever driving, and it comes down to you versus an animal that's run into the road, it's the animal. I don't ever want you to slam on the brakes and wind up sacrificing your life in order to save a squirrel's."

In awe of the cat's agility, I murmured, "That cat saved itself." My heart tossed a penny into a stream. I wished on it that I could outrun minivans as stealthily.

"If you ever kill anything with the car," said Dad, "just consider it a sacrifice to the gods of our ancestors."

I contemplated a Mesoamerican man dressed in feathers and skins wrestling a cat lady's beloveds on top of a pyramid. Their claws dug into his potato skin arms. They ripped stripes into his flesh and pecs. Pomegranate globs dripped onto stone. The sun, a visual vampire, grinned. He was wearing sunglasses, like he did in certain cereal commercials.

"Hey," said Dad. "Did you know that the Maya invented the concept of zero?"

"I don't like math," I answered.

"Neither do I," said Dad. "But I love subtracting cats."

Mom and Dad are both dog people. They made this known on the Fourth of July, after the last sparkler had faded and a sea breeze whished through our front yard. It rustled Mom's black and white hair. It lifted firework ash off the driveway slab. The powder blew to the loquat tree and sprinkled it over the roots.

I felt kind of bad for Dad. He was going to have to wait another year to play with explosives. He was the only one allowed to light our fireworks, and like taking out the trash after tearing everything open on Christmas morning, you had to clean up a lot of shit after Independence Day, too. Dad was doing this. He was crawling on his hands and knees, reaching for burnt up things that smelled similar to Mom's cooking. He tossed a black clump into a wet garbage pail. It plunked.

As Dad had touched flames to fuses, my heart had beaten woodpeckerly. The anticipation of an accident, that this might be the moment my father became one-handed, made me almost whiz my pants. I'd have to wait another year for that same kind of rush. Right now, Dad was no better than a dog trying to figure out where to go. Crawling. Sniffing. More remains plunked into the pail.

Mom uncrossed her arms. She breathed in and out, and I was glad none of my friends were here to comment on her velour high waters. Her glasses reflected garage lights but she was staring at the moon. In Spanish, she crowed, "Look. Look at the pretty moon."

Antonio, Ixchel, and I looked at it.

"Where's the man on the moon?" asked Antonio. "I don't see him."

I looked for him, too, but only saw mozzarella. "He's gone," I agreed.

As chunks plunked into the pail, Dad mansplained, "Many cultures don't see a man on the moon. The Aztecs didn't. They saw a rabbit. So did the Chinese." Scooping up something crispy and holding it up to the moonlight, Dad added, "The Chinese are the reason we can do this. They invented fireworks." Dad looked at the sky. He joined us in moon-gazing.

"Can you guys see the rabbit on the moon?" Dad asked.

The rabbit instantly materialized.

"Yes! Yes!" I shouted. "He's right there!" I pointed. In my moon frenzy, I shouted, 'The Aztecs spoke Nahuatl!"

Watching *Indiana Jones and the Temple of Doom* had inspired me to begin digging a hole in our backyard, a hole that might puncture the earth's molten nickel core and penetrate a royal tomb. After watching me excavate for a week, Mom had surprised me with a gift. She handed it to me as I was coming out of the bathroom, wrapped in a towel. I'd just showered the archeology off of me.

"Here," she said.

"What's this?" I asked, looking at the book.

"Read it. It'll make your abuelito happy to know you're learning about Mexican culture."

I carried the book to my bedroom. I sat on the carpet in front of my closet and set the thing on my lap. It was simply titled *The Aztecs*. Instead of getting dressed, I dripped and read the whole thing. Lingering on the glossary that began with the word Agave, I decided that someday it would be my job to plunder whatever was left of Moctezuma's capital. Flipping back through the pages, staring at the aerial map of Tenochtitlán, the metropolis's precise topography burned itself into the part of my imagination responsible for adventure. So did Tenochtitlán's caste system. I imagined bumping into an Aztec wearing a ponytail, heavy facial jewelry, and feathers. I would say to him, "'Scuse me, warrior."

I imagined a boy wearing a wooden collar and cowering. To him, I whispered, "I won't hurt you, slave."

All roads led to the Great Temple of the Blue Hummingbird, and there I'd encounter Snake Woman, the best-dressed man in Mexico. The emperor wasn't the real HAIC, Snake Woman was. With incense and fresh blood spatter spicing the air, we'd encounter one another at the top of the highest pyramid, where all the satellite dishes were. Snake Woman would be toiling in a hallucinatory state, his breath rank with 'shrooms. His left hand would be tugging a human heart from a rib cage. He'd hold it up for the hungry gods to admire.

"They did speak Nahuatl," said Dad. "Where'd you learn that?"

"Mom gave me a book about the Aztecs. Are we Aztecs?" My pride surged in anticipation of his answer.

"Sorry," said Dad. "We're Chichimecas."

I scrunched my mouth. I asked, "What's a Chichimeca?"

Dad laughed. He asked, "You really want to know what a Chichimeca is?" he asked.

I nodded.

"The Chichimecas are the sons of bitches. The Dog People."

Son of a bitch, I thought. I wasn't telling anyone I was a Chichimeca.

"I'm a son of a bitch?" I asked.

"Daughter," said Dad. Mom laughed.

"Son of a bitch sounds better," I said. "And that's no so bad. The Aztecs ate dog. They ate Mexican hairless dogs. They fattened them with corn and beans, and roasted them for special occasions, like Thanksgiving."

Dad mumbled, "I think we've eaten dog a couple of times."

Mom said, "If you think my cooking tastes like dog, you can cook for yourself."

"I wasn't talking about your cooking," said Dad.

"Whose cooking were talking about then?"

"Your mother's."

Mom said, "It's time for bed."

Mom walked Ixchel, Antonio, and me inside. We brushed our teeth, took turns peeing, and changed into our pajamas. I climbed my smooth bunk bed ladder and slithered onto my mattress. My big toe tapped the Japanese paper lantern hanging from the ceiling. Round, puffy, and water-soluble, it lit our pink room softly, making it feel like a uterus or the inside of a satin-lined jewelry box.

The Aztecs, a diary incapable of keeping secrets, and a plush brontosaurus were lined up on a shelf behind my pillow. Grabbing the diary, I flipped to an empty page and attacked it with my mechanical pencil. Originally, this book had been secure, its red strap locked with a key but the key wound up in the same place half of our socks did: a purgatory in another dimension. With a steak knife, I'd hacked the strap off so I could keep documenting the things that mattered.

In it, I wrote, *July 4th. We had fireworks. There is a rabbit on the moon. I saw him. I believe I am an Aztec not that other thing. Son of a bitch. Son of a beach. That's how mom says it.*

I wedged the pencil back between the pages, shut the diary, and replaced it. I grabbed my brontosaurus and *The Aztecs*.

Light flickered on and off. I turned to see who was doing it. Mom was standing in the doorway.

Flailing my limbs and writhing, I screamed, "Terremoto!"

In a terrified voice, Ixchel yelled, "Stop it!"

Mom said, "Stop it. That's not funny." I wondered how flat my sister would get if my bed fell on her during an earthquake. I could excavate her.

"Mom," I asked, "why is the rabbit on the moon?"

"I don't know."

"Really?"

"Really. I don't know."

"Well, can't you make something up?"

Mom sighed. She said, "His mother put him on the moon because he wouldn't go to sleep."

I asked, "Can we get a rabbit?"

"No."

"Why not?"

"Because we don't need one."

"I need one."

"No, you don't. I don't see you carrying out any scientific experiments."

I giggled. "I'll get out my chemistry set tomorrow. Did you do experiments on rabbits?"

"Yes."

"In Mexico?"

"Yes."

"Why?"

"I was studying pharmaceutical chemistry, and we used rabbits to help us learn about antigens."

"What's an antigen?" I asked, while imagining Dad saying, "It's the opposite of an unclegen."

Mom said, "I'll tell you later."

I said, "Tell me what you did the rabbits."

Mom walked over to me. She held out her hand. She said, "Give me Napoleon."

I handed my dinosaur to her. She held him as if he was going to buck and stroked his long neck. Then, she wrapped her hands around an invisible syringe and pressed its needle to the side of his head. Her thumb pushed the plunger, sending make-believe creatures into a host.

I asked, "Did it hurt them?"

Mom said, "It doesn't matter. It's better than injecting people."

Mom handed my inoculated doll back to me and walked to the doorway. She flipped off the lights. The room turned into an unlit tomb.

Mom cooed, "Dream with the angels."

I reached under my pillow, pulled out my hot pink flashlight, and yanked the covers over my head. In my chrysalis, I opened *The Aztecs* and flipped pages till I found the Aztec calendar wheel. My finger stroked Rabbit, it dug in the space between Deer and Water, and a bolded caption explained that Aztec timekeepers spun their calendars in cycles of misfortune: thirteen. I flipped some more pages and found the rabbit again, this time as Ome Tochtli, god of intoxication.

Ome Tochtli got me drunk on fatigue and my eyelids fell, the flashlight slipped out of my hand. I was transported to Easter Eve in *Tenochtitlán*. *Snake Woman was creeping through the streets past midnight, a large wicker basket dangling from his scarred forearm.*

What was he doing?

Tiptoeing from vegetable garden to vegetable. Crouching in the vines and squash blossoms. Tripping over rabbits and turkeys. Hiding severed human body parts among big red tomatoes for noble children to hunt and roll down pyramid steps at dawn.

Columbusted

On the playground under the slide, during recess from a catechism class where a nun was preparing a bunch of other bored children and me to receive a Jewish carpenter into our mouths, I was conducting my own Ash Wednesday services. I was wearing my red stretchy pants that Dad said made me look like the only kind of trustworthy Mexican: the masked wrestling kind. In my chubby hands, I cradled an ashtray I had whisked off a dyke nun's desk. I dipped my pinky in it. The cremains of the sister's cigar felt satiny.

A dark classmate approached. She shut her eyes. My finger reached for her and smeared Christianity's favorite letter upon her brow: t. Christians dangle this letter from chains around their necks. They erect this letter in front of their churches. It's always lower case.

"En el nombre del padre y del hijo y del luchador Santo," I blessed my classmate. I kissed her on the mouth. I have always been a queer high priestess.

Pedophiles must've surrounded me at catechism but they didn't touch it first: I touched it first. I Christopher Columbused the apple of my loins. It itched bad and I understood that a señorita scratches her papaya in private because I'd only ever seen boys — small, medium, and large — touching their privates in public, and so, alone in my vulvar bedroom, I shut my door and went to town.

In the middle of one particular scratch fest, the tip of my nose itched. I wrinkled and twitched it but the tickle stayed. I unplugged my hand from my figgy pudding, pulled my nose, and discovered that a perfume brewed where I split. I dipped back for more and sniffed. My hand travelled back and forth, back and forth, back and forth from nose to genital cleft, and the smell's ability to regenerate seemed bottomless. I had struck a lucky abyss. I rubbed myself and huffed my fingers until the cows came home. I became pleasantly chafed. The hairnet-wearing cholos who crouched behind my elementary school's handball courts with paper bags mashed to their faces, eyes crossed, could not out-sniff me.

Toting a laundry basket, Mom barged in. My hand wasn't down my pants but my eyes were crossed. My nostrils were flaring against my knuckles. Mom threw her stuff onto our dresser and marched up to my ecstasy. She grabbed my hand. Whiffed. Her eyelashes popped out of their follicles.

"Cochina!" she screamed.

Mom's judgment didn't discourage my huffing. It only made me more circumspect about it. More lady-like. More señorita-ish.

I cliqued up with the cholos behind the handball courts.

The Time I Rewrote the First Couple of Pages of *The Bell Jar* from a Melodramatic Chicana Perspective and Named It *The Taco Bell Jar*

It was a crazy hot-ass summer, the summer a bunch of raza almost killed Richard Ramirez, and I didn't know what I was doing in Guadalajara. I get stupid when I think about Ramirez's ilk: serial killers. What they're called makes me imagine soggy Cheerios, and he was all anyone wanted to talk about when they wrote me letter:. Did you hear about how Richard Ramirez gouged out this person's eyes and hid them in a jewelry box? Did you hear how he raped some old bitch? Did you hear how this one guy survived but they used up all the yarn in the world stitching him back up? Richard Ramirez was never going to dice me, but since everybody was obsessed with it, it made me start wondering what it would be like to be stuck with him in a van with tinted windows. That must be how carnitas are made in hell.

Anyways, Guadalajara sucked mango ass. By noon, the Mesoamerican humidity that rose up from the mestizaje throngs made me feel like I was back in my mom. Moist. Unnecessarily fetal. Exhaust from a billion buses and taxis made cobblestones blur, men wearing clown makeup juggled hollow coconuts at intersections, and the smell of poorly refined petroleum didn't quit in my nostrils. It raked my throat and left gray skid marks.

I kept reading those letters since I missed home. Then I'd think serial killer, cereal, cereal is American, I am American, I eat cereal, I eat cereal serially. Seriously. Reading those letters also took me back to the first time I saw a dead body. It was my cousin's. People at his funeral were whispering that he got murdered. I stood near his casket, waiting for a moment when everyone was too caught up grieving to notice me. Once they were, I reached in to see what his corpse felt like. His cheeks felt below room temperature, which is very wrong.

I knew I was going bonkers that summer because I could not prevent dull but morbid streams of adjectives from flowing through my head. I wanted to dam up *decaying, drowning, graying, putrefying, wilting,* and *molding,* but they flowed and flowed and grew and visions of my cousin's corpse chased the words. I was just so moist and hot and ready to stab myself in the head to get rid of language I didn't want there. I hadn't packed any shorts but I should have. Also, ghosts had begun flapping inside me.

I knew there were bunches of girls who were jealous of what I was doing, and I was so excited before I left that I even thanked the Virgin for my acceptance letter even though I don't believe in her. When my picture came out in the magazine along with the other girls who got picked for the internship, all of us with hibiscuses in our hair, everyone said, "How romantic! Girl writers in Mexico wearing flowers at their temples." How Frida.

"Look what can happen if you pray hard enough to the Virgin," a bunch of people said. If you pray hard enough to her and beg her and grind your teeth as you beg and threaten to become a slut if she doesn't let you win that summer internship at *Chisme* magazine, she will be forced to give it to you. It pays to be an aggressive Catholic.

However, once I got the prize, I wasn't sure if I wanted it. I rode from my hotel to the editorial offices to the parties and to the dinners with those words that I could not shut off. I should have been all *oh my god* about it like most of the other girls were. Instead, I felt like all the hummingbirds in me had died. The hummingbirds responsible for joy and language and sanity had ants crawling on them. Eating them. These hummingbirds that had used to beat inside me now beat ghost wings. They had turned me into the wrong kind of birdcage. A coffin for feather and bone.

Hummers

You can't spell swan without dick. These birds have been acting out since ancient times. The Greek gods took their form to rape girls and did this because the swan lifestyle inspired them. It's a form of divine thug life.

Recently, in Chicago, a gang of swans flipped a man's kayak and aquatically jumped him. Five of them held him underwater until he quit struggling, and then their feather fingers let go and they watched him float to the surface. The most King Kong among them opened his wings like a post-fight cholo boasting, "That's right! That's right! That's what's up, *bitch!*"

Swans aren't the only animals that should've been kept off the ark. Bigfoot was intentionally kept off the ark. Noah and his family worried about having a cryptozoological creature with such big feet on board. You know what they say about hard-to-find monsters with big feet. Their feet stink extra badly.

On Noah's ark, they had dolphins, sea monkeys, and clams. They had calamari and canned tuna. Noah's wife brought Miracle Whip and when the tuna behaved badly, Noah flashed them the pseudo-mayo and raised an eyebrow to remind them of his family's tuna salad recipe.

It's a good thing Noah decided to save the clams. Otherwise, the world would have no women. Clams usually get their periods around age twelve. They loll in the ocean and then, *pffff*, the water they live in takes on a cherry Kool-Aid hue, and the clams are ready for feminine products. Their monthly excretions enrich the water. They make it salty and tangy, like a glass of Clamato. Clams are disembodied private parts. Some are hairy. Others are smooth. Some have hard shells and others don't mind the barnacles growing all over them.

According to high schoolers, monkeys are the worst. Having sex with one will give you AIDS. According to many sixteen-year-olds, AIDS comes from monkey sex which these teenyboppers will tell you is sex with an ugly person, not necessarily somebody with monkey DNA. The DNA can be human; the face, pure lemur.

Some stray cats are into masturbating on women's doorsteps. It makes them giggle to cat-come on a lady's welcome mat.

A lot of animals rape. Dolphins get the most credit for being gang rapists, but raccoons are pretty deviant, too. One time, these two college students were hanging out at a gay male college student's apartment when they heard what they thought was a cat fight in the parking lot out front. They listened to screeches and hissing until it bordered on hell sounds. The college students ran outside but only saw asphalt and cheap sedans under the parking lot lamps and moonlight. No warring cats.

They listened and heard feral noises coming from their left. They followed the pavement down to the edge of the first floor and turned left again. They stood on their side of a cinderblock fence and knew they were near the sound-makers. They looked up to the roof of a shed with dried pine needles creating a highly flammable mattress. The friends saw a male raccoon, wearing a little rapist mask, holding down a female of his species. She was squealing. He was holding onto her furry shoulders and plowing her with fury. Her opera-gloved hands flailed and she lurched forward, trying to escape, disrupting needles, but her rapist had the gift of tenacity. The lesbian college student felt terrible. It felt terrible to be in the moonlight, looking at the profile of a small mammalian rape victim, and her friend screamed, "Stop!" at the male raccoon.

"Yeah!" the girl echoed. "Stop!"

The gay bent over, reached for a pinecone, and pitched it at the rapist. It struck his side, he let go of his quarry, and she bolted away.

The gay whispered, "Do you know what the scientific name for raccoon is?"

"What?" asked the lesbian.

"Procyon lotor."

"That sounds like another word for rapist," said the lesbian. The friends felt shaken, not stirred, by the nature they'd seen.

The lesbian went on to have other horrible experiences with animals. Once, a rabbit made love to her leg. That wasn't so bad.

The lesbian got a girlfriend who was a white person, and this white person got to have an offbeat experience with her school's ecosystem. The white girlfriend was going to community college and was taking a break from her geology class, standing by some Monterey pines with a gaggle of smokers. A rabbit was lunching near their feet, nibbling at taxpayer-funded grass. The geology students admired the animal's innocence till a hawk swooped into their line vision. It extended its talons and used them to lift the rabbit by its nape. It was like watching a more violent version of that game you can pay a dollar to play in order to navigate a claw that grips and lifts a stuffed animal that can becomes yours as long as you don't drop it.

The hawk ascended with its Easter prey dangling, and he rose toward the clear sky, disappearing into pine branches. Since most of those watching were native city slickers, they panicked. Their community college campus was as rural as it got. One of the students whipped out her phone and dialed 911.

"A rabbit's been attacked," she said. The others could tell that the dispatcher was asking a question. The student answered, "A hawk... Hello?"

Something white, red, and beautiful fell near the students' feet. They looked. From the grass, the rabbit's head stared at them, like Marie Antoinette's or Jayne Mansfield's. It was as if the rabbit's bloody neck was now attached to the earth and it was part animal, part celestial body.

The event made the campus paper. The headline read HAWK ATTACKS RABBIT. STUDENT DIALS 911.

This story is verifiable but there are unverifiable hunches some community members harbor about the hummingbirds that live in this same city. One person, who shares these hunches, gardens irregularly. She lives in a blue Spanish style home with one tree, a very fertile guava, in its front yard. Around the guava grow astral succulents, cacti thin and fat, and native California brush such as manzanita and Mexican sage.

It was while trimming the Fremontodendron that the gardener developed her hunch regarding her local hummingbirds. The Fremontodendron had put her in a bad mood. The Fremontodendron, also known as flannel bush, which the irregular gardener enjoys reimagining as a lumberjack's crotch, releases a botanical dandruff that causes itching, sneezing, and eye-watering. The gardener was feeling the itch, cursing the tree, and hacking off one of its branches, which had grown so far into the driveway that it minimized parking space, when she saw the tiny, energetic bird.

It stuck its beak in twixt sage flower petals. Instead of a sipping sound, the irregular gardener heard a snort. She set her hatchet down on the dirt and watched the sniffing bird more closely. It nervously bobbed from purple flower to purple flower, snorting. With each snort, the freneticism in its body multiplied till it seemed liable to explode like the space shuttle Challenger. Then the gardener realized, *This hummingbird has a drug problem. It's sniffing cocaine.*

Each morning, from her dining room window, she watches this overly energetic bird return to the Mexican sage to do lines. It snorts at the flowers, becoming more and more trembly and darting. She puts her ear to the window screen and hears the bird humming cumbias. That is how she deduced his place of origin. He is Mexican, like the gardener's mother and her mother's mother and her mother's mother's mother and her smother's mother's mother, and so and so forth.

Last weekend, she watched him remove a tiny parcel from a flannel bush flower, carry it in his beak to the guava tree, and wait. A nervous sparrow with twine in its beak arrived. The sparrow deposited it on the guava branch beside the hummingbird, and was then allowed a sniff of white powder that the hummingbird arranged on a twig. A blue jay came offering string, set it down beside the twine, and he was allowed a sniff done off the hummingbird's beak. A pelican came all the way from the coast offering a shoelace, which he placed with the rest of the payments, and then he did a toot. After nearly a hundred birds visited the hummingbird, the drug hummingbird took the payments and fashioned a drug mansion out of them way up in the highest boughs of the guava. He hired six crows as bodyguards.

"Pollen" allows the hummingbird to be all he can be. *Hummmmm…*

Petra Páramo
for Abuelito

    In the forest lived the ghost of a girl who knew very little. She knew for sure that she was dead. She knew for sure that she was a girl since gender is something that you just know. People know what their gender is the same way that they know whether or not they are dead or alive or prefer cake to sugar cones.

    The other thing the ghost knew and was absolutely sure of is that all the best things to come out of México have come out of the state of Jalisco. Beyond those certainties, the ghost existed in the form of doubts. Everyday, her doubts sprang leaves, vines, and stubborn buds. Questions. *What's my name? What kind of music do I like to dance to when I dance alone? How many languages do I speak? How did I die? How many books have I read? Am I a virgin? Did my mother want me? Did my father love me? Did I love him? Are there other ghosts? When will I be old enough to shave?*

    She wondered if she had died in the forest where she lived. She did have one memory, but she wasn't sure what it represented. Thinking about the memory moistened her slippery brain. In it, she looked up at a circle of light filtered through grayish water. Maybe she'd struggled at the bottom of a well, a drowned girl. Maybe she'd been flushed down a toilet. Maybe she was remembering being born. The ghost thought it was most likely that she had drowned but wasn't sure. As was said earlier, she was certain of very few things. She wasn't even sure what certainty meant. She knew things, but didn't know things with a capital K and that capital K was very enticing to her.

    Cotton clouds were marrying and divorcing in the sky above the redwoods. The ghost was squatting against a trunk, gazing up, playing a game she played most afternoons. Her eyes darted, seeking ghosts among the nimbuses. Her curiosity scrutinized each puff. Foggy snakes drifted.

    Are any of you ghosts? she thought, her mind telepathically signaling this question at the sky.

Brutus! her brain dubbed a choppy cloud.

Sylvia Plath! her brain dubbed a smoky one.

Nobody, her brain dubbed a boring puff. Nobody is the name of most ghosts.

She wondered about the ghosts of her mother and father. For all she knew, her mother and father might be Brutus and Sylvia Plath. However, she doubted they were. She did have a hunch that her parents were dead which meant that she was an orphan. Staring at the cloud she'd named Nobody, the ghost reasoned, *All orphans are not ghosts, and all ghosts are not orphans, but everyone will be a ghost someday.* This logic made her smile. She thought, *Everyone will be an orphan someday, too. This means that all orphans are ghosts, but only in the most future tense sense of the word.* She quit smiling. She felt sad for everybody and nobody and Nobody.

More than anything, more than any animal, mineral or vegetable, the dead girl longed to know more than what she did. It sucked to only know a pocketful of things with a capital K, and the ghost wished to be able to fill a drugstore notebook with facts that she could prove with charts, tables, and anecdotes. She had a feeling in the pit of her deceased stomach, a feeling that sentences shouldn't end in a preposition, and so, as she wished, *Man, there's so much I wish I could be sure of...* she felt insecure about *sure of...* The clouds melted into a single serving of mashed potatoes.

All I know, the ghost ruminated as she traced the hole where an umbilical cord had once tied her to someone, *is that I'm dead. I'm a girl. And the best things to come out of México came out of Jalisco. Mariachi.* Trumpets blared in her head. *Tequila.* Alcohol poured into an imaginary glass. *Charrería.* Cowboys lassoed black and white stallions. *Pedro Páramo.* Ghosts flew out of the pages of a book, their dead hands and hooves tickling and galloping along her invisible gray matter. *Did I even make it to my quinceañera?* she wondered. *Was I a mariachi prodigy? A female rodeo star? Do I like to read? Am I even literate? Do I suffer from any food allergies?*

The ghost continued tracing the spot where her body had been tethered to her mother's. Her gaze remained fixed on the clouds. She identified and sorted some according to flower, two resembled peonies;

celebrity, one danced like Michael Jackson; and various foams: sea foam, cappuccino foam, bubble bath foam, and rabies foam.

The ghost sort of knew that if she wanted to learn anything about her origins, how she died, or how to program a VCR, she'd have to leave the Christmas-scented place. Brooding beside ferns, she'd considered stowing away in a camper's vehicle, crouching invisibly beside a cooler stuffed with brie, seedless grapes, granola bars, and crackers. The idea of riding in a car made her skin break out in goosebumps. It seemed too much like flying. She had no memories of having ridden in cars and enjoyed walking on loam, especially on rainy days, and gazing up at the blue and the white and the pointy treetops. The ghost decided *If I'm going to leave the forest in search of knowledge, I'm doing so with my own dead feet.*

Honey sun lit the ghost's walk out of the forest, and she stopped to admire plants, animals, and smells. Pausing at her favorite redwood, she put her face to it. Its bark clawed her cheeks. She sniffed it doggy style. She pressed her eyes so close to the wood that she could see its texture change from one red to another red to a cousin of that red, a collection of tree bloods. She licked the giant. The tree tasted of nothing. She had hoped it would taste like a holiday.

Hugging the tree goodbye, the ghost turned and continued walking. A fallen bird's home appeared in her path, and she got down on all fours to examine the light blue eggs cupped by nest. Her sixth sense told her, *The babies in the shells have no heartbeat.* She used her sixth sense to holler, "Hello!" at their ghosts, but looking up into the arms of the oak they'd plunged from, she only saw a bitch-faced mockingbird, a flesh and blood one, scowling down at her. Sometimes, animals sense ghosts. Not all of them do, but certain animals are particularly keen about it. Mockingbirds possess this talent in spades. So do salamanders and molting iguanas.

The curious ghost lifted her hand. This walk out of the forest was meant to be a learning experience. With her fingers I-have-a-question-high, she smacked her palm down against the nest. *Crunch!* sounded. Shells cracked against her skin, jags digging into her useless lifeline. Splaying her fingers, the ghost stared at her destruction. "Scrambled eggs," she mumbled. "I just scrambled eggs."

Yellow and pink screamed life and death, and goo coated the crunchy nest. Red bits swirled the gold. Twigs, hay, grass, a speck of light blue glass, and pink string punctuated the scramble. Baby bird eyeballs floated, caviar.

The ghost's stomach growled for what she'd made. She wanted to put it in her mouth and eat it, but human taste is the one sense that the dead are denied. Instead of eating the mash, the ghost did the next best thing. She shut her eyes and inhaled the scent of the would-be birds and their home. Her invisible marrow pulsed. She was savoring the smell of their destruction. She smeared her hand down her side, marking her nightgown with her accomplishment.

She said, "Hey, baby birds, when I was alive, I might've been dropped from a tree, too. Maybe that's why I'm like this. Maybe we're related by mode of death."

The ghost stood up, and the sudden knowledge that she might not see any of these plants or rocks or animals again smacked her. She began bidding everything farewell out loud, "Goodbye, heart-shaped rock. Goodbye, playful fern. Goodbye, random shrub. Goodbye, berry-filled pile of dung. I wonder if those are wild raspberries..."

Her walk slowed as she kicked through a California golden poppy colony. She wondered, *Do poppies exist outside the forest?* Freezing, she sank to her side, and felt flowers tickle her check. She relished using flowerbeds as beds. From her worm's-eye view, the world was all poppy, only orange petals and doily leaves. She shut her eyes and fell into a totally unnecessary nap.

The ghost opened her eyes to thin green stripes. Stems. She scrambled into a half-up position. Leaning on her hands, she peered around. The moonlight was glowing extra neon for her, and she stood, stomped her feet, and wiped the wrinkles from her nightgown. Faint purple flowers dotted it. It was the only piece of clothing she owned but she didn't mind. It felt soft and really let her move. *Let's go*, she thought.

She continued wandering towards what she believed might be the edge of the forest. Once she got there, it was indeed the edge of the Christmas-scented place. Its trees gave way to something probably never-before-seen: farmland.

This earthscape unfolded in gray squares. Strawberries sprouted from white plastic covered rows in some. Grapevines stretched and coiled in others. A sour grape fell silently into the dirt. The palest chunks of farmland were lying fallow.

"Ooh," whispered the ghost. "So unwoodsy."

She tiptoed onto an unsown patch. She expected the earth to fall away from under her, but it didn't. The planet didn't turn to ash or mush as she abandoned the only place she sort of knew. Dirt remained strong and held her. The unknown was real. It was strange that places where she had never been (or had she?) were real. She wondered, *Is this what death is like for people who've just died? Does it feel strange?* Death felt familiar. Her ignorance about most things also felt familiar to her but she was sick of this particular familiarity.

She walked across wild grasses cows had munched to stubble. She floated through barbed wire fence and laughed. She hardly ever used her ability to pass through things because it felt like a cop out, like, *oh gee, I'm dead, I don't need to honor the organic, let me float right through that boulder,* but it seemed funny to her to float through something that would've killed her if she was meat. It made her cackle not to get cut or tetanus. "Ha-ha-ha!" she boomed. "Barbed wire fence, you fail!"

The ghost crouched so that her mouth was parallel to the fence's second wire strand. She parted her lips and her non-existent tongue snaked out. It licked metal. It tasted of absence, nothingness, but triumph beat its chest inside the ghost. She could lick fatal things and not suffer any consequence. She could pick up a poisonous frog, lick it and not die. She could eat a bag of AIDS-infected needles and not choke. All these dangers would taste the same, like the number zero, but they could never result in her demise. In death, the ghost triumphed over all earthly dangers.

"What a trip," she whispered and tried to imagine what the barbed wire tasted like. She figured it probably tasted like a mouthful of pennies. She seemed to recollect sucking on a mouthful of coins and felt like, yes, there was a moment in time when she had shoved coins in her mouth and sucked on their flavor. They tasted poor.

"Nothing can keep me out," she said. "Barbed wire. Fences. Muskets. Flame throwers. Nazis. I can go wherever I want." This feeling of being able to go wherever she wanted gave her self-esteem balls.

The ghost walked along dry grass and onto a two-lane road. This strip was a dark shade of dark by day. By night, it offered a screen that moonlight bounced off. The ghost figured this would be as good a road as any to follow so she continued her walk along the asphalt, which felt warmish against her feet. *It must be summer,* she thought.

Oak looked like wild things against the purple horizon. Stars were pretending to be diamonds. The clouds had all gone home. An owl spoke into the night. The night returned no echo. A cricket chirped one note. Things rustled in the trees and grasses. The ghost felt around in her soul. She was looking for fear. She couldn't find any. Nothing could kill her. Perhaps she could kill. Perhaps she had killed.

The ghost followed the moonlit road up and down slopes and dips. She savored her solitude, introspecting, wondering, until she heard voices. She wondered, *Who the heck is out here?*

The talking was coming from over the hill. The ghost scampered towards the source, and got within slapping distance of two girls walking down the middle of the road. They held hands and shared haircuts, identical bobs, except one girl's bob was curls while the other's was not.

Lovers? wondered the ghost. She kept close. Her ears perked up.

"I swear," said the straight-haired girl, "I think that thing that bumped into my head was a bat."

"Bat's have really good sonar systems," argued curls. "I don't think a bat wouldn't notice that you were right there and just crash into your forehead. Your forehead's not even that big. I think a bird hit you."

"No, I saw it right before it hit me in the head. It was clearly bat-shaped. I know bats. My favorite book is *Interview with a Vampire*. A bat crashed into my head. Did you ever hear about how if a bat flies into your head, it can cause your hair to fall out? I read that in a library book. It's a superstition, but what if it's true? I could wind up looking like Captain Picard. If that happens, nobody will ask me to the prom."

Curls sighed. The girls continued their talk about bats, high school, a recent mountain lion attack, their school's dress code, shoes, and how awesome it would be to become vampires. The ghost caught hope shimmering in the head of the girl who believed a bat had struck her. The girl was wishing, *Tonight might be my lucky night. Maybe that was a vampire, and it bit me super lightly, so lightly I couldn't even feel it, and I'm going to turn! I won't have to go to school on Monday.*

After tasting this thought, the ghost realized that she *could* taste; as a ghost, she wasn't completely denied this sense. This sense, however, manifested in being able to taste brainwaves. She experienced flavored mental telepathy. The vampire thought left a medium rare and silly taste in her dead mouth, the way it tastes when you cut your index finger as you're mincing celery and decide to suck it.

The girls' conversation stumbled to a lull, and the ghost dipped into the other girl's head. She was thinking *I hope my best friend and my sister aren't dyking out.* These thoughts tasted heavily of wishful thinking. Curls *knew* that her best friend, the girl that she was strolling with, was indeed fooling around with her sister. She'd never caught them making out in her sister's Ford Ranger, but the looks they exchanged as their hands reached for the same nacho after school at Taco Bell said more than enough: Sapphists.

The trio headed up and down slopes and dips. The night smelled the way only California can by dark. It also felt alive because of the stars, owls, and coyotes debating whether or not to pounce.

The ghost thought, *Coyotes. Roadrunners. What happens when a roadrunner runs through a ghost town? Why are ghost towns called ghost towns? Isn't a town a town because people live there? So then shouldn't ghost towns be called a ghost something else?*

The girls had resumed their conversation, describing how awesome it would be if they could be undead, if only they could find a vampire willing to turn them, and they rattled off places where such a creature might be found. They believed he — and he had to be French — lurked with taste and sophistication at bars, nightclubs, symphony halls, and smoking rooms. The one who'd been struck in the head said, "I'll bet vampires can't get AIDS."

The road bent. The ghost made out the shape of a white mailbox. It stood at the mouth of a dirt lane stretching to a farmhouse. The girls turned at the mailbox and muted themselves. They moved towards the house. Curls grabbed the back door's knob, turned, and pulled. The pair tiptoed inside, and the girl who was still in fear of her hair falling out shut the door behind them.

The ghost wasn't interested in passing through the door to follow the girls. She found them kind of blah and felt that the information they had to offer wasn't the kind she was looking for. She thought, *I want to taste the minds of more mature people, the elderly, those with one foot in the grave. The wise.* The ghost had a sense that the knowledge she lusted after might be historical, genealogical, theological, or, perhaps, even occult. The ghost looked to her left. A smaller house stood about an acre away. She thought, *Why not?*

Moving her feet, she left the farmhouse behind. She traipsed through a dark acre and its fuzzy vines tried to trip her. Long curly leaves tickled her ankles. Her legs brushed swelling gourds. It was a Halloweeny minefield.

Nearing the house, the ghost decided to do like a living person. Instead of floating through its front door, she prowled the periphery of the one-story home, eyeballing windows. Along the backside of the house, curtains billowed beyond a sill, their cotton fingers poking and pointing, and the ghost walked over. Her ankle grazed a garden gnome. His magic acknowledged hers, and he fell over, doing a face plant. The ghost ignored him. She wasn't into gnomes. She pressed her palms to the glass and pushed up the pane. Curtains reached for her, masking and blindfolding her face. She blew back at them and jerked her head, freeing her eyes. Shifting her hands to the windowsill, she hoisted herself up, crouched, and dropped, landing on a carpet whose color the darkness kept from her.

She could see the outline of a TV on a cart. Beside it, a potted plant. A glass coffee table hung out in the middle of the room, and an overstuffed couch and loveseat L-ed around it. No ottoman.

The ghost bopped to the media center. A record player rested on its middle shelf. A record collection standing on the top shelf threatened to betray its owner's tastes. The ghost waited till her eyes adjusted to the special darkness of a stranger's living room at two in the morning. Then, she pulled a record off the shelf.

"Dan Fogelberg," she read aloud. "Never heard of him." She replaced the LP and ran her hand along the record player lid. She lifted her finger to her eyes to see how dusty it was. It was too dark to tell. Dust shared the same hue as most other grays in the room.

Snoring. Someone was sawing logs close by. The ghost turned and followed the ugly sound out of the living room, past the moonlit kitchen, and down a cramped hallway. She stepped through an open doorway and into a room where a queen-size bed was backed against a wall. Behind it, the room's biggest window. Where she was standing was like putting a conch shell to her ear. Oceanic. The snoring broad was a white lady enjoying a waterbed.

The ghost walked to a chair in the corner. She parked her bony pompis on it. She folded her hands in her lap. She gazed upon the sleeper.

The snores that unfolded from the sleeper's mouth were sharp and wet. She gobbled up air like it was going out of style but then choked on it. Moonlight beamed down through a skylight directly above her face. The ghost stared at the lady's features, guestimating her age. Bunches of lip lines and papery neck skin told that she was probably sixty-something. Her short gray hair might've once been chestnut. She snuggled in a plaid nightshirt. The ghost glanced at her nightstand. A half-empty glass of water and gold hoop earrings. She glanced back at the lady. Her eyeballs twitched against scrotal eyelids. The ghost reached beyond her gray hair to taste her dream, to savor its meaning or lack thereof.

The lady was dreaming about a woman she knew, the volunteer coordinator at the hospital where she lent her Saturday afternoons. The snorer's brain hid the volunteer coordinator's mini-biography in a mental attic. The ghost reached for the attic door's dangling rope, yanked it, the trap door fell, and the ghost crawled in. In the musty black and white space, the ghost found the knowledge that the volunteer coordinator had come of age as a Belgian Jewess named Françoise. When the Nazis invaded, they took Françoise's parents to be cooked while she and her brothers and sisters ran. The Nazis hunted for them, so, as the oldest, Françoise made up her mind that it would be nobler for her and her brothers and sisters to die by their own hands than by Nazi ovens. She was huddling with her siblings behind a train station. Sweat was plastering her shirt to her underarms. A rivulet leaked from her jewfro. It slid down her forehead and cried down the bridge of her blunt nose.

"We are going to find a place where we can sleep forever," she told her brothers and sisters. "Help me to find the bridge."

The orphans shuffled away from the depot and wandered through nightfall, searching for the right jumping spot. They spotted a curving one that was both high and pretty. Their shoes clopped along its stone, to its highpoint. None of them knew how to swim, and Françoise had picked up her youngest sister and was holding her over the river, about to toss her in, when a finger tapped her shoulder. Françoise turned to see who was interrupting.

She looked into a freckled face. The freckled pest asked, "What are you doing?"

"Dying," Françoise admitted.

"Why?"

"We are Jews."

The freckled pest glanced around the bridge to make sure they were still the only ones on it. She saw no one else, but chose to whisper anyways. She asked Françoise, "What if I hide you? What if, in the name of Him, I hide you? Will you not commit this sin then?"

"Who is He?" asked Françoise.

"The father, the son, and the holy ghost," she answered. "I'm a nun."

Françoise looked the nun in the eye. She promised, "If you hide us and we live through this, I will give myself to your Him."

The nun led Françoise and her brothers and sisters to her nunnery. She herded them to a barn in back and hurried them to a wooden ladder. They climbed it to the hayloft. The kids lived through the war there, nibbling turnips and parsnips, reading books about the lives of saints, peeing in buckets, drinking straight from cows' udders. When the war ended, the kids came down from the hayloft, and Françoise took her vows (she also made a silent vow never to eat -ips — parsn- or turn- — again). As a wife of Jesus, Françoise changed her name to Sister Barbara. Instead of dangling a crucifix from a thin gold chain around her neck, she hung a silver Magen David. It sparkles as she yells, "You're late again!" at hospital volunteers.

The ghost sighed with satisfaction. The information in the snoring lady's head had tasted of precious metals, miracles, and olive oil. She thought to herself, *This is why I left the poppies behind. To get to chew on stuff like this.*

The ghost wondered if what she was gathering by entering the snoring lady's mind wasn't just knowledge but wisdom. She felt unsure. In the morning, she'd have to find a dictionary. She wanted to be sure of wisdom's exact meaning.

The ghost slid back into the snoring lady's head to taste her actual dream. This event layered like lasagna noodles across Sister Barbara's backstory. In the dream, the snoring lady was wearing a blue jumpsuit. Motor oil stained her knees. She sat, legs hanging apart, on a chrome and red leather stool. She held a cone piled high with chocolate soft-serve ice cream. She licked her Gene Simmons tongue up the side to the tip.

In that way that only happens in dreams, where you just know that one thing is another, the ghost understood, *the soft-serve was Sister Barbara.* The ghost giggled.

She continued eating the lady's dreams. As the sun rose, and its rays really lit up the lady's face, the ghost wondered, *How many of us watch the living sleep?*

Once hearty daylight took over, the ghost rose. She crossed the bedroom and traveled back through the cramped hallway to the living room. She could now see that the lady dusted often. Spider plants spilled out of pots in all four corners. The ghost glanced at the glass-topped coffee table, at the magazines splayed across it. One, two, three *Time* magazines. A *Readers Digest*. A *Catholic Digest*. A box of Kleenex. A matchbook.

She heard stirring coming from the bedroom and headed for the window. She hopped outside, and landed back beside the fallen gnome.

A fox was prancing along the northern edge of the pumpkin patch that the ghost had crossed the night before. Sensing death's presence, the fox quit her morning exercise and stared. When the ghost sensed the fox sensing her, she waved and called out, "Hi!" to the fox.

The fox coiled her head back, a little shocked by the upbeat greeting, and kept her eyes on the non-existent girl. The ghost kept going. The fox watched her trample daisies, crunch across front yard grass, and pace to the road. She stepped onto its sandy shoulder and walked, feeling pebbles tickle her feet. Talc-y dirt.

The fox looked down at its shadow. Her plump shape reminded her she was pregnant. She resumed her morning exercise.

The ghost headed in the opposite direction that had delivered her to the chocolate soft-serve dream. Daylight made the oaks look more real. Scrub jays dueled around mossy strands dangling from their branches. A fluffy tarantula sidled along the pavement. Thoughts of what a tarantula might taste like kept the ghost busy for one, two, three, four, fifteen miles of parched canyon. At the twenty-second mile, the road bent, bent again, and at the proceeding bend, it cut through very thirsty grazing land framed by gray-brown cliffs. Near the jags, thirteen mostly white people stood about at a smattering of boulders and rocks. One of the ladies was holding her hand to her forehead, blocking the sun. She stared across the road. The ghost followed her gaze.

It landed on a man standing beside a parked yellow school bus. He was shoving his finger down the heel of his shoe, fiddling with his sock. The ghost looked back at the rest of the people.

I'll bet they're trespassing, she guessed. The rocks and boulders formed a natural semi-circle around a dead cypress tree weathered ivory smooth. The tips of its leafless branches were blackened, as if they'd been struck by lightning. Votive candles and flower bouquets littered the base of the trunk and the rocks. On the biggest boulder, vandals had spray-painted a pink human heart.

A balding man knelt, facing the cypress. He clasped his hands in front of his chest. He bowed his head. His silver watchband glowed. His bald spot shone. The ghost dipped into the brain of the lady watching the man by the bus.

"Come on!" she called out.

In the lady's brain, the ghost groped her way to a mushy little tabernacle.

She pulled open its meaty door to find herself sitting on a pew, facing an altar with a sexy crucified Jesus hanging behind it. A white lady wearing green polyester pants and a yellow shirt polka-dotted with bingo dauber stains was addressing an audience of twelve. A priest was sitting off to the side, supervising from his armchair. The lady teetered on the shag-carpet, shifted her stare from a stain to the parishioners, and proclaimed, "I had a vision! A woman with a sword appeared in the sky over Alamoc Canyon! The blade was shining, and she pointed it at the ground. She threw it into the dirt beside a cypress tree that was crispy at the tips! I *know* that this woman I saw is the Virgin. She has chosen us for something special! Who would like to go to this place in Alamoc Canyon and pray with me?" she asked.

Every attendee's hand shot up. Growing Catholic gangs had been making fieldtrips to the spot for months. The ghost could hear the murmurings of the pilgrims' hearts, *Virgin, help my son find a job. Virgin, help a job find my son. Virgin, we can't afford braces. Can her teeth get straightened by accident? Virgin, make my husband stop spending so much time with the neighbor with the huge chichis. Virgin, give me the winning lottery numbers. Virgin, who is more important: you or god?*

"Come on!" the lady yelled at the guy again. The straggler's hands moved along his temples, smoothing his black and silver hair. His hands fell to his pants pockets, and he looked at the lady. Lifting his knee, he sprinted towards her. Canyon winds stirred. Their *whwhwhwhwh* muffled the grumbling semi turning at the blind spot. It careened at the straggler and its grill slammed his hip. He erupted everywhere. Burning rubber smell and horn sound wrung every other noise and smell from the air. The Catholics froze. Body parts hailed and slapped the pavement. The pilgrim's foot landed on its sole, by the ghost's toes.

Somebody wailed. The ghost thought, *Pilgrim's lack of progress*, and felt tingling in her invisible veins: she knew she was mentally referencing a book! She felt certain of that but she had no idea who had written the book, what it was about, or why she knew about it. Frustrated by her knowledgeable ignorance, her nostrils flared. A medley of screams came from the Catholics. Fate was treating them to a vision of sacrifice. Now they knew exactly what it was like to watch someone get hammered for their sins. It wasn't just a metaphor anymore. *Now maybe they'll realize how important patience is*, thought the ghost.

The driver monkeyed down the side of his rig. His blonde mullet bounced behind him. Landing on the street, his eyes darted from piece to piece to ambrosia salad of the man he'd hit. The ghost sensed his desire to run in the direction of his victim but the circumstance paralyzed him: his victim was everywhere. He would have to resign himself to visiting the parts of the whole.

The ghost stepped over the foot. It was wearing a civil oxford shoe. Its fresh stump exposed bone, marrow, sinew, and vein. The ghost's foot landed in blood, and it clung to her see-through soles. As she headed south, dainty red tracks showed up in her wake. A lone Catholic dude noticed and watched their creation. The footsteps soon faded, becoming nothing.

The Catholic dude wondered, *Are those footsteps Anacleto's? Is that his spirit walking out from the wreckage?* It did not occur to him that the footsteps might be a virgin's. But after all, weren't the pilgrims there for a virgin's sake?

The ghost jogged to the new spirit. She tilted her head back to look up at his face. He was pursing his lips in an O, watching his aftermath. Her invisible veins sizzled with jealousy: at least he had answers. He knew how he died. He knew why. He might even be able to create jokes about his own death. Why did the Catholic cross the road? He had eternity to work on his punch line.

"You're dead," the ghost informed the new ghost.

"Yes, I figured that out," he said.

"How do you feel about it?" she asked.

The new ghost pondered the question. He said, "At least I won't have to listen to my wife scream at me anymore. She's a really good cook, though, and I'll miss her food. Especially her puto."

"What's puto?"

"A Filipino dish. Rice. Say, do you know how I can get some food around here? I'm starving."

The ghost rolled her eyes. Then she reminded herself, *Patience*, and explained, "You can't really eat food like you could before you got hit by a truck. Most things taste like nothing, but people's thoughts are sort of our food. They have flavors. You can taste what living things are thinking and feeling, but they aren't normal flavors. Like, something might taste like joy, but it won't taste like chicken. Well, it might taste a little like chicken. You can taste the weirdest stuff, like apathy, disgust, love, and procrastination. Anything that's in a living thing's mind can stimulate your spiritual taste buds." The ghost looked down at her toenails. "Sometimes, though, you can't get in touch with your own self. Like, I can totally know everything about anyone by going into their minds and scrounging around but I don't know how I died. I don't know my name. I don't know how old I am or how long I've been wandering. I feel uncertain of almost everything. My grasp of stuff is slippery. All I know for sure for dead sure is that I'm a girl, I'm dead, and the best things to come out of Mexico came out of the state of Jalisco."

The new ghost laughed. "Sounds like you're biased," he said.

The ghost raised her eyebrows and said, "That's what knowledge is. An extraordinary bias."

The new ghost smiled. He said, "That's something different to think about but for right now, I'm going to go with my death. It was nice meeting you." The new ghost smoothed the hair at his temples and sprinted in the direction of his insides and his outsides.

The ghost watched him over her shoulder. *People can be so weird*, she thought.

The ghost continued her walk out of the canyon. A fire truck with sirens and lights going squawked past. Its speed ruffled her nightgown. A fleet of police vehicles followed by an ambulance sped past, too. Their velocity blew her hair into her face. More and more vehicles zipped to the extravaganza. The ghost didn't care about them. She cared about the aged eucalyptus trees coming into view. They shaded clapboard stables. Upon their wood-slat fence, a grizzled donkey was resting his chin. His black jellybean eyes watered, and the ghost wanted to pluck them and eat them. She floated across eucalyptus nuts. Apostrophe-shaped leaves mentholated the air. The ghost stretched her unseen fingertips towards the donkey's muzzle. Her knuckles slid down his fuzz.

"Velvet," she said. "You're so velvety. And your eyes are very, very pretty."

The ghost dipped her sixth sense into the donkey to see if he, too, was thinking of velvet. She was greeted by a mental image of him as a young stud mounting a white mare. His thighs pumped against her hindquarters.

The ghost's cheeks heated up. The donkey purred. He rubbed his cheek against her hand. The ghost plunged her fingers into his coarse black mane. She wanted to taste his hair. Leaning towards it, she opened her mouth and sucked. Flavorless.

She pulled away. A spit string connected her to the animal till it snapped. The ghost petted the damp mane as the question *Should I or shouldn't I go to the town those impatient weirdos came from?* bandied around inside her.

"I'm on a knowledge quest," she whispered into the donkey's ear. "I want to know stuff. You know that expression 'you don't know shit'? That's me. I want to know, like really know, so much I could fill a spiral bound notebook or two thousand. I want to pig out on knowledge."

The ghost smelled the ghost of donkey lunch. Its warmth wafted towards her. She peeked around the donkey's neck, at his rear hooves. Fresh road apples comingled on the dirt. The donkey was helping the ghost to know shit. She giggled. She kissed the donkey's nose and stepped away from him. She crept back to the dirt shoulder and walked.

More and more cars filled the road, and then the road branched into roads. A looping overpass spanned a four-lane highway. Cars zooming along kept decent safety spaces, and rigs corralling oranges, peppers, and garlic hauled past. A green truck leaking white feathers barreled along. The ghost sniffed. Chicken shit.

Near a freeway off-ramp, families were laughing on AstroTurf. They swung clubs, trying to putt golf balls out of mazes. Beside the mini-golf course, houses that looked like one another, white stucco tract homes with red tile roofs, were crammed together.

The ghost floated across the freeway and walked along a white fence. A Dutch windmill cast its shadow across her, and she gazed into the sky. The sun still lit the world but the moon had also taken her position as queen. Due to this mutual occupation, there was no difference between night and day. Lavender ribbons sailed in the sky above the mini-golf course's glaring triceratops statue. Orangey vanilla bursts streaked across the roof of the nearby hotel. Plump palm trees in a pumice pebble river made the lobby entrance look prehistoric. Splashing. Chlorine. People were playing in the hotel pool.

Funky pepper trees lined the sidewalk leading towards traffic lights. The ghost walked along the sidewalk. She headed past Randall's Feed and Supply, the Paradise Motel, the Sandpiper Motel, the Indian Motor-Lodge, and Refugio's Tires. Mexican markets with signs you had to know Spanish to understand. The ghost trotted towards a windowless structure whose red and white sign announced FRUTAS Y VERDURAS.

By FRUTAS Y VERDURAS's automatic doors, a coin-operated merry-go-round with ponies painted in primary colors sat hungrily. The grinning yellow horse matched mustard but reminded the ghost of lemons. Her deceased salivary glands pumped sadness into her mouth. *Papaya*, she thought, *give me a papaya*. Anger quivered her lips, and she floated towards groceries through FRUTAS Y VERDURAS's tinted glass door.

Her feet touched down after the black plastic doormat. The shellacked concrete floor felt chilly. Fluorescent lights lit the frutas y verduras in an otherworldly way. The sight of pink, yellow, orange, pale green, and brown peels and rinds caressed the ghost's spirit. She'd eaten these things — these fruits, vegetables, grains, and tubers — before, and her invisible marrow did back flips. She knew she'd eaten radishes that went crunch, and white hominy that soaked for days, and potatoes and carrots that turned tender and forkable in massive pots. Someone somewhere had placed plates of chirimoya and biznaga and coriander and chiles poblanos on a table in front of her. Memories of taste revivified: she hated mole. She knew she hated mole as sure as she knew she was not alive. She especially hated mole poblano. Why ruin meat with chocolate? Don't let them play together. Dessert deserves her own throne, her own plate, her own spotlight. The ghost felt confident that in another time and place, she had eaten mangos and papayas till they gave her tropical diarrhea. She had eaten bolillo and birote drizzled with red sauce. She'd eaten sopes and huaraches and tunas, not the Chicken of the Sea but the chicken of tree, prickly pears to throw at people you hate: teachers, landlords, and dentists with big hands.

The ghost walked to a stand piled with guayabas, their bubblegum smell taunting her, and she crumpled beside their ripeness. Her lower lip wobbled. Her hands clutched at her nightgown. They bunched it, and scrunched it, and twisted it. A wave of mortal hormones crashed over her nonexistence. Tears sprang and wended down her cheeks, marrying at her chin. Her ducts replenished their streams each time it seemed there shouldn't be any more non-existent water inside her. She squinted through the wetness. Colors swirled into a pretty gob. Her cheeks bunched. Her chin dimpled. Grief burned her tongue. Trembling, she heaved as she wept.

Nearby, a clerk was minding the register. He licked his finger and turned the page of the magazine on the glass countertop. His eyes moved along gossipy sentences. Pictures of Argentinian soap stars with mortgaged cleavage. A fly landed on his register. It reached its arms to its cheeks. Groomed its chops.

The ghost lifted her hands to her cheeks. The feeling of her own touch was soothing. She kept her hands on herself and felt the tremors wracking her growing weaker and softer. Weaker. She rocked but coaxed the rocking to slow. The movement vanished. Her tears ducts ran out of water. Her face stayed warm and slick. She moved her hands down to her neck, letting the warmth toast her fingertips. She remembered the guayabas. Her fists rubbed her eyes, and she blinked. She blinked. She blinked. The fruits came back into focus. The guayaba closest to her nose would be rotten by morning. She reached, grabbed it, and clutched it to her chest, between her never-to-grow boobies. She breathed on the fruit which had no effect upon it, her breath was inorganic, immaterial, and she sensed the wannabe life in the fruit, the multitude of seeds, some gay, some lesbian, some straight, some of infinite other sexualities. She blew on the round thing and jabbed her finger into it. Mushiness ate her invisible skin, and she pushed her finger through, through, and through the fruit's axis, till it emerged on the other side. With the guayaba impaled, the ghost laughed like a woman. She flicked her arm forward. The orb sailed and hit the concrete, splatting and spraying its insides.

The clerk looked up from his magazine. His bored expression remained unchanged. Fruit fell from the stands all the time. Lemons avalanched. Oranges rolled down small orange mountains. Coconuts bowled gutter balls. Sometimes ghosts were the culprits behind these fruity hijinks but often the laws of physics were responsible. The clerk scurried around the counter with a terry rag. He picked up the guayaba and ran the cloth over its puke. He carried the mashed fruit to a metal trashcan and held it over the mouth, letting it drop. It landed with a wet clunk. The fly took flight, sailing towards its dessert.

The ghost tilted her head back. Her gaze pointed heavenward. Instead of Saint Peter, paper mâché idols floated above her. A Dora the Explorer piñata and a cross-eyed Winnie the Pooh piñata and a bootleg Cinderella piñata conga'd from a wire. The ghost sucked in air and blew at them. A cowboy piñata's fringed chaps danced. The clerk looked up to see them rustle. His eyes darted about to find where the breeze was coming from. His expression turned from bored to confused to *hey, wait a minute…*

The ghost stood, straightened her nightgown, and turned. She thought, *There's no point ogling these fruits if I can't taste them.* She walked towards the automatic door. The glass sensed her. It acknowledged that they shared a virtue: invisibility. The clerk watched the door slide open and shut for no one. His daughter's name breathed into his mind. *Is that you, Selena?* his conscience asked in Spanish. *If it is, I'm sorry I didn't do a better job of protecting you from your mother.*

The ghost stood under the fist-pumping arms of a half-naked pepper tree in an auto parts store parking lot. The sun had left the sky entirely to the moon, and the moon was enjoying this. The moon was smiling, and the ghost said to her, "I see you. I see you smiling."

The moon said nothing back but gave delicious minty moonlight. Her whiteness refreshed the ghost's mental palate. She savored that astral glow, basked in its maternal influence.

"Will you be my mother?" the ghost cooed at the moon.

Her pelvis leaned against the hippie pepper tree trunk. The tree's body was the opposite of the ghost's. The ghost's stretched straight and lithe while the tree's was verging on third trimester. The tree was a woman, as much as Helen of Troy and Kim Kardashian are women with capital Ws, and, yet, the ghost paid no mind to her physique. She rarely thought about what she looked like, though she had wondered, *If I ever see a portrait of myself, will I recognize it?*

The ghost kept asking the moon questions and listening for the moon's answers. She didn't expect to get one but her ears perked anyways. Occasionally, along the road behind her, headlights whooshed up a lane. As last call came and went, drivers wove and drove into oncoming traffic. The ghost ignored their drunken antics. She was vibing with the moon. She was reaching out to her heavenly aura.

"Okay," said the ghost. "If you won't be my mother, then will you be my sister?"

Again, the ghost breathed lightly, waiting for her answer. Parking lot dirt, pepper tree leaves, and bottle caps buttressed her feet. Near her little toe, a crushed Tecate can. Rainbow confetti leading to a smashed egg. A poopy diaper someone had tossed out of a backseat.

The night's warmth held the ghost. A sense of everything being so beautiful that it must be destroyed squeezed her. Stars impersonated opals. A comet shot in an arc over the roof of the auto parts store, and a tiny green dot glimmered, becoming part of an unknown constellation, vanishing.

"Aliens…" whispered the ghost. Her body shivered. Her muscles released a virginity into the universe. She was experiencing an orgasm. It had been inspired by awe.

The ghost asked the moon, "If you won't be my mother or my sister, will you at least be my friend?"

The ghost narrowed her eyes at the moon. She fluttered her eyelids. She was intentionally blurring her eyesight so that the moon nodded her assent. A breeze lifted the ruffle at the bottom of the ghost's nightgown. This breeze tickled the inner parts of her knees. The moon was saying yes to friendship.

The ghost awoke in a tight space that reeked of the pound. She yawned and stretched but her arms banged wood. Light streamed through a horseshoe hole, and the ghost crawled through it and onto a patio. She turned around and saw a sun-blanched red doghouse.

"I was in the doghouse!" she gasped aloud. She turned to see a white mutt with black spots squatting next to a kibble-filled bowl that read KILLER. The mutt cocked its head and stared at the ghost. It barked, "Arf!"

"Why was I in your house?" the ghost asked the dog.

The dog answered, "Arf!"

Remembering that the moon had promised to be her friend, the ghost asked the moon, although she'd gone from the sky, "What was I doing in the dog house?"

In her mind's eye, the ghost saw herself from outside her own body. She was leaning against the woman-tree in the parking lot of the auto parts store, and, as if under a spell, she stared up at the moon. She nodded at the heavenly body, became a vessel for lunacy, and walked off the dirt island onto the tar. She sleepwalked across the black, across rows of empty parking spots, and through a chainlink fence. She walked the cement till her invisibility bumped against a doghouse. In imitation of a black bear, she crouched, crawled into it, and hibernated. This three-month cooling off period had been a gift from the moon.

"Thank you," said the ghost.

"Arf!" said the dog.

The ghost flung her arms open at the sky. She drank sun for breakfast.

"Arf!" the dog cried again. The ghost wanted to kick him in the mouth. He scampered to gravel ringing the concrete and crouched. The corners of his hairy lips turned up. His tail rose. Urine shot onto the pebbles. The ghost stepped through the peeing animal, pulled open the gate, and stepped onto thick dark green grass. It poked between her toes. She shuffled along this carpet, happy to feel a bit of the forest in this town or village or whatever it was.

She wove through a mint green condo complex, across front lawn, and onto a sidewalk covered in hopscotch squares drawn in pink chalk. The ghost lifted one leg and hopped from box to box to boxes to box. Landing in the final square, she resumed use of both her feet.

At the corner, she stepped into a crosswalk. She journeyed deeper into the stupid heart of wherever she was.

The sights were typical. Of no consequence. McDonald's. Sammy's Spirits. The Hotel Broadway. The Greyhound bus station. Memo's Zapatería. Jones' Boot Shop. A-OK Furniture Rentals. Wong's Szechuan Cuisine. Arco gasoline. A park with a wooden gazebo and a frothing waterfall. The Hap E Daze Retirement Community. A sky with no stories to tell. Just a color with a pretty name. Cerulean.

Breezes whistled at the ghost the way fuckers in trucks whistle at females of all ages. At times, the breezes whispered more than they whistled, and the strongest breeze of all — the breeze that picked up sycamore leaves in the gutter and played with them, swirling them into a cyclone — made no noise. The ghost watched these dirt devils with shrewd eyes. They reminded her of nature's evil nature. They reminded her that the clear sky above her was a lie, and that the sky and everything under it could have potentially murdered her.

"*Whwhwhwhwhwhw...*" she called back at the wind.

Signs nailed to a three-story building's boarded up windows read For Sale or Lease. On the next block, Botánica San Miguel and Botánica de Allende flanked Mama's Thrift Shop. Through Mama's windows, the ghost saw dark-skinned women pushing recycled shopping carts down clothing-stuffed aisles. Both botánicas reeked of incense, candle wax, and small-time juju. These obscured the smells emanating from Mama's. A neon sign blinked in San Miguel's window. One letter at a time, it announced P-S-Y-C-H-I-C R-E-A-D-I-N-G-S-C-O-M-E-O-N-I-N. The ghost paused and stared at the green and purple words, letting the sign repeat its message several times before making up her mind. *Too predictable,* she thought and kept going.

A Presbyterian church and City Hall and hearty magnolia trees blossoming in well-trimmed squares of grass. Behind their polished leaves, a concrete sign announcing City of Ayulas Public Library. *This,* thought the ghost, *is IT.* She visualized herself sliding the perfect hardback off a shelf in the occult section. She imagined hugging the book to her ribs.

She imagined understanding herself. The ghost thought, *There will also be beanbags!*

She set out across the lawn. Magnolia seed maracas lay here and here and there. She kicked these out of her way and traveled under the eaves. An automatic glass door swung open, she entered, and she dillydallied by the seaweedy carpet that ended at the circulation desk. She gazed to her right, at the entrance to the children's section. Behind glass, in a display area scooped into the wall, a paper-doll diorama of Maurice Sendak characters danced around propped up copies of *Where the Wild Things Are* and *In the Night Kitchen*. Huge Sendakian butcher paper trees slouched at the tunnel-like entrance. The ghost felt compelled to head over there. God, it looked fun.

She looked to her left. Boring, but probably a wiser choice. Everything about the grown-up area seemed a few steps away from purgatory. Plenty of uncomfortable seating. Fabrics permanently defiled by bodily odors. Caca-inspired earth tones. Signs fixed in place with yellowing scotch tape. People who looked like ghosts but were not. Reading material. The ghost headed into the grown-up area.

Since it was noon on a Wednesday, the people patronizing the library were those with the time, or need, to be there. Leathery men in ball caps skimming jobs classifieds. Ladies talking to themselves and unseen companions. Folks with AARP cards in their wallets. Stay-at-home spouses. Flashers.

The ghost passed through a wide doorway and saw *Vogue, Seventeen, The New Yorker*, and more magazines resting face up on display shelves wrapping the walls. Shelves jammed with books filled the center of the room. A sign suspended over them by fish wire read FICTION. The ghost curled her upper lip in a sneer. Since she was in search of knowledge, fiction could lead her astray. Fiction was a lie. She turned left, ran past the elevator door, and mounted the stairs two by two. The staircase curled in a series of squares, and the ghost gripped the railing to make it easier for her to move her short legs across big space.

Arriving in Nonfiction, she took stock of the reference desk, the shelves to her left, and the tables. At one, a man who couldn't recall the last time he'd combed his hair stared at the sports pages he held close to his glasses.

The ghost crept towards the shelves, shelves crammed with serious reading choices, no fiction, no lies. Glorious nonfiction. She ran her fingers down spines that announced geological titles, horticultural titles, botanical titles, and architectural titles. She touched these books about plainly physical things, and snaked up and down the stacks till she arrived at selections that were about things as invisible as her. The metaphysical. The philosophical. The theological. The spiritual. She found these books and more at chin-level and stroked their spines with her knuckles. "Hmmmm," she purred. "Hmmmmm…"

She yanked Immanuel Kant's *Critiques* from its shelf. "Critiques," she said aloud. "I like it. It sounds bitchy."

She carried the *Critiques* past the bathrooms and into a reading room with microfiche readers on one side and a wall-sized county map on the other. The ghost sat diagonally across from the table's only other occupant, a man dressed as if he'd survived Armageddon. He rocked to his own beat. His eyeballs stared forward but couldn't see what was in front of them. They were only able to look inward. His eyes darted at the ghost. He looked her in the eye while staring inward.

"Hi," she told him. "I'm here to read." Curiosity tugged at her. She really wanted to know what was going on in her neighbor's head. She wanted to know where his rhythm came from.
As she poked in through his nostril, a baby's orphaned screams blasted her right out of his head.

She didn't know what to say, and was too spooked — yes, ghosts can get spooked — to ask why that noise filled him. She decided the best thing was to pretend she hadn't heard shit. She looked down at her book and opened it to a random page.

She placed her finger against a word and read: Synthesis, generally speaking, is, as we shall afterwards see, the mere operation of the imagination — a blind but indispensable function of the soul, without which we should have no cognition whatever, but of the working of which we are seldom even conscious. But to reduce this synthesis to conceptions is a function of the understanding, by means of which we attain to cognition, in the proper meaning of the term.

The ghost looked up from the page, at the ecru wall. She thought, *So John Lennon was right: Imagine.* She imagined herself back in the forest. She imagined eating and tasting bananas. She imagined eating and tasting meatloaf. She imagined milking a brown goat. She imagined finding blood in her underwear. She imagined blowing out fifteen candles. She imagined herself reflected in a mirror. She imagined herself with a heartbeat. She imagined herself as the unimaginable. She imagined she had Yoko Ono's hair. She imagined herself kicking a ball.

Deep in the hominy of her soul, the ghost knew — *knew* — that though she found soccer drop-dead boring, she was still definitely Mexican.

She whispered, "I'm dead. I'm a girl. The best things to come out of México came out of the state of Jalisco. *And I'm Mexican!*"

Looking at her neighbor, she hissed, "I'm Mexican! Are you?"

She waited for his answer. Emboldened by this important morsel, the ghost snaked back up her neighbor's nostril and into his memory bank. Again, she heard the baby wailing. She swung from the tree branches of his mind. The green was dripping with chunklets of dead Vietnamese people. She could hear the man crying for them. His sobs had a guilty melody. The baby's wail screeched out of a cave. Its wails vibrated the trees. It wailed in the man's dreams.

"I'm sorry," the ghost said to him. "I'm sure that if that baby's ghost could talk to you, it would tell you that everything is okay because someday, you'll be a ghost, too."

The ghost noticed his beard moving. Lice were tooling about. She squirmed. She thought, *I'm dead. I don't need food or water or clothes or a nice bath, but he does. And nobody gives it to him. Living people are awful. Who cares if his brain is full of jungles and dead babies? Every baby will die someday. He was a baby one time. Even Caligula was a baby.*

The ghost felt her nightgown for pockets. She knew it had none but even ghosts are susceptible to wishful thinking. She wanted to give the man spare change or nuts or berries. She wanted to push something nourishing across the table to him. It shamed her that she had nothing to give him.

She turned back to the book. She flipped to a new chunk. She read: There exists in the faculty of reason a natural desire to venture beyond the field of experience, to attempt to reach the utmost bounds of all cognition by the help of ideas alone, and not to rest satisfied until it has fulfilled its course and raised the sum of its cognitions into a self-subsistent, systematic whole.

The ghost's mind summoned a black hole.

She returned to the text: Is the motive for this endeavor to be found in its speculative, or in its practical interests alone? *Hmmmm*, thought the ghost.

Text: Setting aside, at present, the results of the labors of pure reason in its speculative exercise, I shall merely inquire regarding the problems the solution of which forms all other aims but partial and intermediate. The highest aims must—

Pee-pee. The ghost couldn't hear it but she smelled musky ammonia. The man was peeing himself. His shoulder trembled. The smell of three hundred and sixty-seven showerless days suddenly became too much for the ghost's nose. That was how long it must've been since her neighbor had last bathed. She thought, *I Kan't do this.*

Looking at the man, she said, "I'm so very sorry for your existence."

She abandoned the *Critiques*, walked around the table, and stood next to the man. She leaned in towards his cheek. Right above his beard, she kissed him. Into his ear, she whispered, "If somebody lights you on fire for fun and you die of the burns, look for me. I will be your friend. But I cannot be your friend in your current form." She kissed him once more and then walked away from him, the portmanteaus, "Mexikan, Mexikan't, Mexikan…" repeating in her mind.

The ghost was loitering al fresco. Near her, two twenty-something white women dressed in t-shirts cut to expose their armpit hair were ranting. Frustrated by the library, the ghost was taking a more anthropological route. She'd hoofed to the café across the street and stationed herself at a bistro table. She was going to sit and listen to caffeinated people talk. She was going to engage in the coffee-driven culture of the living.

"Here, I finished reading this," one hairy woman said to the other. She pulled a pamphlet from her burlap purse and set it on the tabletop. The other woman grabbed it. She said, "Thanks. You were right. It's hysterical. Loved it."

"I knew you would. People flip out over the S.C.U.M. Manifesto but it's, like, Valerie's just taking misandry to a hilarious extreme. I mean, it's an inverse of how men treat us."

"Yeah. Fuck men." The man-hater took a bite of cream cheese and bean sprouts on wheat toast. "Fuck that guy who mooned me the other day."

"You got mooned?"

"Yeah. I was in the parking lot at hardware store after picking up some caulk, and this guy without a shirt, he just had on short shorts and a sweatband, was jogging laps around the lot. He smiles at me, jogs in place, turns around, bends over and shows me his flat ass. I could see his pruney little ball sack dangling, begging to be chopped off."

"What did you do?"

"I yelled, 'Stay that way so I can run you over with my car!' "

They snickered together.

The one who hadn't been mooned was wearing a sports bra. The fabric under her pits was toasted golden. Her pit pelt ran silky and straight.

The ghost tugged her nightgown collar forward and peered down into her armpits. She discovered freshly sprung hairs! Maybe she was like these women. Maybe she was a man-hater, too. She thought, *Maybe I oughtta snatch that pamphlet.* She continued eavesdropping and felt that their conversation was way more enlightening, fun, and useful than that Kant book. She also realized that the women might not like Kant because of his first name, Immanuel.

The woman eating the sandwich talked about getting her haircut at the mall. As she'd sat in a salon chair getting shorn, she'd lusted after her bisexual hairdresser, Genet. She told her friend, "Genet's like a Nagel painting come to life."

"Meow."

"I wanna bend her over and show her who's boss. Also, I caught two kids doing it in the stairwell over by Carl's Jr. I guess the smell of charbroiled cow is an aphrodisiac for little straights."

"We should go hand out fliers for our consciousness raising group to the girls that hang out there, at the mall, under the clock. Otherwise, they'll just grow up to blindly suck cock."

"Yeah. We oughtta get our hooks into them while they're teenagers before they let the patriarchy fuck 'em six ways to Sunday."

The sports bra-wearer asked, "Do you ever feel like sometimes you laugh at men's jokes just so they won't kill you?"

As the two veered into a conversation of all the things women do to placate men so that men won't kill them, the ghost got up. It was time to hit the mall. There might be girls like her there.

The ghost had seen the mall on her way to the café. She'd ignored it, finding its buff brick façade unappealing but the prospect of kids doing it in stairwells and hypersexualized hairdressers enticed her.

The mall rose across the street from the library. A labyrinthine parking structure surrounded it. The ghost stomped along the pocked concrete trail that led to its ground floor. She was getting a little frustrated with how unexpectedly difficult her quest was feeling, and she floated through the glass doors. She sailed across waxed stone floors and hovered in the wide walkway between Howie's Hoagies and Salon C'est Chic. Odors representing the two businesses dueled. Aerosol hair spray and perm solution fumes wrestled with scents of horseradish and fresh-baked bun. The result was toxic and fin de siècle. Strangely appetizing. It made the ghost hungry for a pastrami on combs.

The ghost was about to head into C'est Chic in order to find out what a Nagel poster was, but she sensed a commotion coming from next door to Howie's, at Tookie's Toys. Stationed in front of Tookie's were two men cut from the same cloth as the secret service. Thingies with curling plastic cords were jammed into their ears and sunglasses shaded their eyes so you couldn't tell their intent. *Is the president shopping at Tookie's?* thought the ghost. *Is he buying a scale model of Earth so that he can improve his international diplomacy?* The ghost decided to find out.

Crap! she thought. *Who is the president?* She decided it didn't matter.

Floating into the store, she hovered across the Monopoly board patterned carpet. She swept to the cash register, where an employee in a red polo shirt and khaki pants stared at a man holding hands with a boy. They were browsing at a wall covered in boxed action figures.

The man's skin was the color of lait au café, which is eight parts milk, one squirt moo juice. His child companion wore an outfit identical to his: a long-sleeved, blue, button down shirt, black chinos, black house slippers, and white athletic socks. Their hair differed greatly. The man wore a wig that gave him a silky semi-mullet. He wore a touch of black eyeliner and pieces of white tape around his right hand's knuckles. A few leftover wisps hung from the child's mostly bald head. He was going through treatment for something, cancer or something like it, and the ghost's sixth sense told her that the man was emotionally feeding off the kid's broken-down state. His closeness to death, his fragility. The man saw himself as a fragile boy and wanted to surround himself with himself — other fragile boys. His ideal would have been to swim in a pool filled with fragile boys, but being a bajillionaire in America can't buy you that. Maybe it can in Dubai.

The ghost got close to the pair. She wanted to hear what the man was saying to the boy. The man turned his face to the boy. The ghost gasped at his profile. Skin, muscle, and cartilage had been sculpted and resculpted and re-resculpted and pulled and tinkered with and rearranged and messed with so many times that his face, especially his nose, was a mess. Silly putty. Also, the ghost was finding it impossible to tell his race. This ambiguity gave her a feeling of kinship with him. She dove into his head to see if she could find out why he'd done what he'd done to himself.

Dance melodies pumped through his brain's stereo system. Neurons shimmied to cutting edge choreography. The ghost tripped on the words *sequin*, *boy*, and *Peter Pan*. A biplane piloted by a chimpanzee flew through the gray matter. A banner waved behind it. It bore the phrase, *Carve the race out of your face*.

"Anything you want," the man said to the boy. "Anything." The man squeezed the boy's hand.

"Okay," the boy whispered back.

The ghost wanted to see what words were sailing through the boy's head. She was curious if he was playing dance music in there, too.

She penetrated a patch of hairless scalp and heard him thinking, "I don't want to die, but I especially don't want to die in his bed. I do want roller skates."

Hmmmm, thought the ghost. *Something funny is going here.* Since she lacked the life experience to understand abusive sexual dynamics between men and boys, her thoughts and feelings couldn't crystallize around her hunch. She knew, by the knot in her non-existent throat, that something weird was going on but she didn't have a name for it.

She felt sad for the carve-the-race-out-of-my-face man. It had taken her getting the gumption to leave the Christmas-scented place and trek through a canyon and into a town and into its library to glean one useful piece of information, that she was Mexican. Here was a man who knew his lineage but was destroying its evidence. Maybe in death he'd wake up with amnesia, too, and because of what he'd done to his face, he'd be unable to recognize the ghost in the mirror. His ghost might have to go on an identity reconnaissance mission, too.

The ghost turned and followed Monopoly properties back outside. She stood at the mouth of the store and stared into mall oblivion. Girls in bicycle shorts and shiny shoes laced with black ribbons ran around in herds, pointing at Tookie's, squealing, "He's in there! I swear to God, he's in there!" Their bangs were ratted into claws, some into full-blown fists, and the ghost ran her hands along her silky but flat hair. *I wish I could have big hair*, she thought.

The ghost floated into C'est Chic, to an empty esthetician's station, and grabbed a hairbrush resting on a stylist's counter. She looked at herself in the oval mirror. Following instinct, she whipped her hair forward, bent her head slightly, and ratted the hair at her bangs and temples. She flipped her hair back, looked at herself in the mirror, and ratted more, till a tumbleweed crowned her. Setting the brush on the salon chair, she grabbed a can of hairspray. She squirted half onto her bush and thought, *Now, I'm up-to-date. I'll feel less self-conscious around those girls this way.*

She and her big hair floated out of C'est Chic, but wanting to blend in with the living, her feet touched down, and she walked. She padded along the waxed floor and stopped after The Futon Shop, in front of Sticky Dogs. Oh my God, what an odor! The ghost ignored the humanity around her, the girl herds in their short shorts and crop tops getting checked out by dads, surfers, grandpas, and security guards. She ignored the mall walkers wielding hand weights. She ignored two nuns in brown habits fishing chocolate chip cookie crumbs out of the bottom of tissuey yellow sacks. Screw all of them. Deep fat fried hot dogs in corn batter were heavenly.

The ghost stared at Sticky Dogs aquarium. Sugar swirled through its lemonade and whole lemons, lemon wedges, and ice cubes bobbed. She placed her hands against the coolness and huffed the hot dog smell. On the other side of the counter, girls dipped sausages in yellowish meal and thrust these, dripping, into fryers. The smell was too celestial, something to trade true love in for, it was so good. The ghost's nostrils fluttered. The part of her that could still experience ecstasy went for it: an olfactory-based orgasm rattled her from the waist down. Pleasure pinged out of her big toe.

The ghost stayed like this, sniffing cooking corn dogs, for one hour, till her invisible body was all out of smell-based orgasms. She opened her eyes to take stock of her surroundings.

The teenage girls were gone. A blonde family was sitting down to snack near the stairs, their teeth biting into corn dog tips. Mall walkers were pushing through their sixtieth lap. A little girl with bouncy, black curls pushed a doll in a stroller towards Ayulas Pets and Pet Supplies. Her mom followed behind her. The ghost glanced right, at the tall clock lollipopping between the up and down escalators. The man haters had said that's where the teen girls hung out, but there wasn't anybody there. Not even escalator riders.

The ghost flew into the air so that her feet hung an inch above the counter. She floated across this barrier, into Sticky Dogs. A white ladder leaned against the lemonade aquarium. A blonde Sticky Dogs employee holding the world's largest swizzle stick was climbing it. Leaning over the side, she dunked in the stick and stirred. Ice cubes tapped the glass and lemons spun in circles. The blonde, corndog-eating dad stared at the Sticky Dog girl. The whole lemons in the tank made the mixture stubborn so she really had to move her whole body to do her job. Her rump jiggled in her red and yellow hot pants. Lemonade splashed onto her hip-length blue top. A conical red, blue, and yellow cap protected lemonade from her stray hairs. Watching the dad's lap pitch a tent, the ghost's cheeks imperceptibly reddened.

Is that what those women at the café were talking about? she wondered. *Will my body ever grow into a spectacle for corndog eaters to stare at while I try to work?* She doubted it would. *As a ghost, do I escape becoming an object?*

The ghost regarded the objects at the food prep station. Two wire baskets filled with lemons. Plastic bags of hot dogs. White vats holding batter. Metal fryers. Most objects here was edible. The girls working there seemed edible, too.

The ghost floated through the wall, into and through Sticky Dogs' stock room and wall, and out into an alley. A man wearing shorts and a short-sleeved buttondown shirt was hauling cardboard boxes down a truck ramp and stacking them near Sticky Dogs' back door. The ghost headed up the ramp and across the truck floor to a corner. She sat, pulled her nightgown over her knees, and waited for the truck to move.

Without any windows to show her the relationship of the sun to the moon, the ghost had no concrete way of telling time. Ghosts, however, have excellent internal clocks. She knew that it was dinnertime when the truck stopped and withering sunlight came in through the door.

A man wheeling a dolly unloaded the last of the cardboard boxes. The place where these boxes were heading pulsed. The ghost's sixth sense felt other ghosts, or ghostlike things, lurking nearby. She crept down the ramp, and followed the dolly-pushing man into an industrial kitchen.

She wandered through its maze of ovens, stoves, and steel shelves stocked with pots and pans, and then pushed open swinging doors and emerged in a cafeteria. Half its lights were out. Four men and three women sat at various round tables, talking across their food trays. They sipped coffee out of Styrofoam cups. One picked at her cuticles. One was eating tater tots with his fingers. A girl in a nightgown sat at her own table. She ignored the meal on the tray in front of her. She stared down at the baby carrots brightening her plate and hardly breathed. The ghost walked to her and sat in the empty stool bolted to the floor beside hers.

The girl did not blink. The ghost wondered, *Is she dead?* She reached for the girl's wrist. Her skin felt cold and goosey. The ghost placed her invisible finger over a vein. A pulse beat.

The ghost liked sitting with this girl dressed like her, but she wanted to talk to her, not cheat by going into her head to gobble up her identity, memories, stories and hang-ups.

"*Psst,*" she whispered to the girl.

The girl kept staring at the carrots. The girl's hair was very thin. She lacked eyelashes. Skin swaddled her skull but lacked fat and muscle to prop up her cheeks. This made her face sag like an experienced person's. The ghost glanced at the girl's hands. They, too, were chicken bones. The ghost wondered if the girl had a disease that ate her fat and muscle, that might make her heart vanish, and she whispered, "Why are you here? Why are you in this place?"

The girl stared at her baby carrots.

The ghost frowned and floated towards two blue uniformed women mopping in a corner. They talked, their heads close to one another's. One looked at the skeleton girl and gestured at her with her chin. The ghost listened.

In Spanish, the woman whispered, "What kind of fool chooses not to eat? That girl, she doesn't eat. That's why she's here. I've heard that when they take her back to her unit, a nurse sticks a tube down her nose and empties liquid into her stomach. If they don't do that, she'll die."

The other woman shook her head and muttered, "Crazy, crazy, crazy."

The other said, "If my daughter ever did that, I'd make her eat." She improvised a martial arts move with the mop.

The other woman laughed and said, "Right down her throat!"

The ghost heard the skeleton girls' loud thoughts, *I understand you, you stupid bitches. I speak Spanish.*

Then the ghost realized, "Oh my God! So do I! I understand Spanish! I'm bilingual!"

An orderly by the door called, "Dinner's over. Back to the unit for group."

The men and women and girl stood, carried their trays to a trash can, dumped their baby carrots, hamburger crusts, leftover tots, and fruit cups, and followed the orderly back through sterile halls. He stood in front of a wall-mounted machine and swiped a plastic card. A buzzer meeped, and he shoved open a heavy door stenciled with the words Chemical Dependency and Eating Disorders, leading the patients through windowless rooms.

They made their way down a white corridor and into a room outfitted with two pea green couches, a table stacked with board games, a ping-pong table with paddles resting on it, and a foosball table. A gray-haired with lady with a curly reverse mullet and wearing billowing batiked clothes presided from her folding chair. Empty folding chairs formed a moon around her. "Welcome to group," she said.

The men, women, and girl chose their spots while the ghost leaned against the ping-pong table. The gray-haired woman folded her hands over one knee and announced, "Today, we're going to do some more inner child work. We're going to keep trying to connect with that inner child. This is that wounded child who lives inside you but she's hurt. You're trying to soothe her with drugs and alcohol and addictive behaviors. That person is in pain and crying. Give that child a voice, a voice that child probably never had when she was growing up. Candice, you're first."

Candice tapped her espadrilled foot against the linoleum. "Pass," she said.

"Alright, then. Veronica." The patients shifted and looked at their laps or stared at the girl. The leader folded her wizard sleeves across her chest and stared down the girl. Aggression emanated from the gray-haired woman. Her lips were already in that phase of life where they were stuck in a frown, but their frown turned further down. Her shoulders tightened. She repeated, "Veronica."

The ghost looked at the clock. 7:30. She looked back at Veronica. Veronica acted exactly as she had in the cafeteria. The patients continued looking at their laps or at Veronica's face. The gray-haired woman stared her down. Candace tapped her toe against the linoleum. *Tap-tap-tap. Tap-tap-tap. Tap-tap-tap.* Ahem. Knuckles cracked. *Tap-tap-tap. Tap-tap-tap.* Nothing. No words. That is the scariest: the sensation of freefalling into communal silence. Communal frustration without a language. *Tap-tap-tap.*

The ghost looked at the clock again. 7:35. She looked back at the group. The gray-haired woman bent her arm, put her elbow against her knee, and rested her ineffective chin on her palm. The ghost thought, *This is the most awkward thing I've ever been through in my entire death.*

She stepped into the gray-haired woman's head. She tasted orange juice from concentrate and the thought, *Come hell or high water, I will get this girl to admit she was molested. I will get her to crack. I know she's been molested. I can feel it in my arthritis. We're gonna pull this anorexic shit out by the root.*

The ghost glanced back at the clock. 7:36. She jumped into the girl's head.

The girl was sitting at a table in a pink kitchen, lusting after movie popcorn, the last thing she'd enjoyed eating. She was thinking, *This is ridiculous. How can I participate in a group about getting in touch with your inner child if I still have an outer child? This is dumb.*

The ghost thought, *She has a point.* She rooted around in the girl's memories to see if she could find proof of anything the gray-haired woman suspected. She dug through wet layer after wet layer but there were no memories, no bad touch there. Just a lot of chemically-induced fears and sorrows. The ghost stumbled into a memory bubble, popped it, and she was sitting with the girl in her floral-papered bedroom. The girl knelt on her carpet, leaning into her long closet. She sniffed at a shoebox on the floor. The ghost leaned closer to see if she was sniffing shoes. She wasn't. A chocolate glazed donut was in the box. The girl sniffed and sniffed and sniffed, only allowing herself to taste the donut through her nostrils. She stuck her nose into the donut hole and devoted every cell in her being to her smell ritual. The girl grabbed the lid and slammed it over the box, shoving the donut back behind more boxes. She crawled into her closet, and crouched under the hem of a white dress. She tucked her short legs against her chest. She slid a pocketknife from her pocket. She flicked free a small blade and held it to her inner thigh. With an automaton's expression, the girl dug the knife into her skin, tracing a stretch mark, turning it red.

The ghost leapt out of the girl's brain. She was tired of experiencing people hurting themselves or torturing themselves or hurting others or torturing others. Maybe she should've stayed in the forest. Maybe her quest for wisdom and knowledge wasn't worthwhile. Maybe it was best to share communal silence in a circle or to carry your silence alone.

The ghost looked out the sliding glass door window. Her friend, the moon, was in the sky again.

"I'm coming," said the ghost.

The moon beckoned the ghost through the yard surrounding the psychiatric unit, along blossoming dogwood trees, down residential streets. The ghost followed the moon's silent chirps, and if one could've seen her, one would've seen a ghost in a trance, a girl in a white nightgown with matching skin and ratted black hair that scraggled to the middle of her backbone. Her face said nothing about her place of origin. Some people might've looked at her and said, "Probably Mexican." Others might have looked at her and said, "We can't tell. She could be lots of things." Still others might have thought she was an escapee from the hospital. She looked hungry, but not for food. Her hunger ran intellectually deeper than that. She wore her appetite on her skin. It completely lacked color. It lacked anything. That absence tainted her, invisible.

The moon quit whispering to her in front of a two-story California Craftsman. All its lights were on and house music shook the window frames. The ghost saw reflections of herself, barely teenaged girls, sharing a cigarette under a front yard bottlebrush tree. She walked up the front walk and let herself inside. She wandered around the house, across Persian carpets and kids barfing into potted ficus trees. Couples made out on leather couches.

She headed up the wooden staircase into the first bedroom on the second floor, where ten kids were sitting cross-legged in a circle. In the middle of the circle, a glass jar. One mushroom remained. The kids were panting, their fungal breath heating up the room. It felt mushroom muggy.

The ghost stood by a frail white desk. Some of the boys and girls in the circle were glancing at each another. Some were staring straight forward, waiting for the drugs to take effect. Two blonde girls acted totally normal, gossiping about girls they considered sluts.

The ghost got the feeling that someone was staring at her. She turned to see if it was a fellow ghost. One of the seated boys was staring directly at her. The boy happened to be black, and wore a red, white, and blue striped polo shirt, jeans, and topsiders. His diamond stud earrings sparkled. His hair was coiffed in careful curls and he sat beside a redhead in a pink on purple cheerleading uniform.

"Oh my God!" cried the boy.

"What?" asked the redhead.

"It's Anne Frank!"

"What?!"

"It's Anne Frank!" he cried again. He pointed to where the ghost was standing. The ghost sweated and felt panicky. She'd wanted to talk to a living teenager and now here was this boy, naming her, but she knew, she just knew, she knew, knew, knew the same way that you know your gender and whether or not you're alive that she was *not* Anne Frank.

"I'm not Anne Frank!" she screamed at the boy. "I don't know my name! Who's Anne Frank? Was she Mexican? How did she die?"

The boy told the empty space, "Well, you're Jewish and I think you died in a concentration camp or something like that. I'm not sure. I learned about you last year in World History. This year, I'm taking U.S.

"I'm not Anne Frank," the ghost said firmly.

"Then why do you look like her?" the boy asked accusatorily.

"I don't know. Why do you look like yourself?"

"Because I am myself."

"Okay. Apply that same thinking to me."

The 'shroomer grew quiet. Kids who'd heard that one of guys tripping upstairs was talking to Anne Frank came charging into the room. They gawked at the space where the boy was addressing his dialogue. The ghost hated having all these fingers pointing at her, people muttering, "I don't see shit… Me either… He's just making it up for attention…" It made her feel like she existed even less so she climbed into the window and jumped.

The hedgerow lining the porch cushioned her fall. She sprang out of it and ran across the street and kept running and running and running. She sweated, her nightgown bunched around her hips, and she ran till she saw a park. In it stood a manmade forest.

While she caught her breath, the ghost thought, *I'll go build a nest there. I'll go build a tree house and stay with the crows and hawks till I've decided whether or not to continue this stupid journey.*

The street separating her from the park was empty save for a dark lump in the middle of it. Walking towards it, the ghost thought, *Roadkill.*

Drawing closer to the lump, she tried to categorize the roadkill. She wanted to know what kind of dead animal she was dealing with. She stared down at a brown paw and still wasn't sure. Whatever had destroyed the thing hadn't run it over or splattered it — it seemed pretty intact — and yet it seemed to be missing a head. The ghost knelt down beside the creature.

She put her face to the dead thing's stomach. Smelling the recently deceased, the ghost realized, *This is special roadkill; this is roadkill that has never been alive.* It was so never alive that it had no face, no brain, no memory, no lungs, and no guts. It was just dead meat, dead meat, dead meat, and more dead meat covered in a mink coat that had always been and will always be unalive. This lump reappears in this same street although crows will fly down from the eucalyptus trees to tear and gobble it down to its ribs. Garbage truck wheels roll over it, squishing it into the asphalt till the thing and the road are one. The dead meat is then reborn as a fresh fluffy lump in the gutter, a fresh fluffy lump by the stop sign, a small body on a speed bump. The first five cars that run it over smell as though they've rubbed down their vehicles with durian fruit.

The ghost placed her hands atop the special roadkill's fur. Feeling it the way a medium touches a missing girl's possessions in order to deduce if her parents should be hopeful or not, the ghost whispered, "Okay, I get it. I'm like you. We're part of the same family. Neither of us has ever been alive. We're beyond that. Our faces are unrecognizable to everyone. Nobody can take our picture because we're beyond human. I was born a ghost. Just like you were born dead. We have no lived experiences. Only dead ones."

She thought her last thoughts in pictures, instead of words. That is the genius of ghosts and animals.

Tzintzuntzan

Like a great religion, my parents conceived me in the desert. Water, however, did serve as one of their earliest aphrodisiacs. Two years before my making, they drove to Michoacán, to honeymoon on the banks of Lake Pátzcuaro. On its shores, cattails rustled, and my parents slid together into a tight canoe that set sail for the island of Janitzio. Fat yellowthroats chirped at Mom and Dad. They could smell that they'd been doing it a lot. Fisherpeople were casting butterfly nets into the water. Dad peeped through his camera lens and snapped a picture of Mom smiling and wearing so much eyeliner it would've made Cleopatra jealous.

On shore, Mom and Dad ate whitefish with heads still attached. As their shadows grew thin and long, Mom and Dad's bellbottoms swished towards the sun. Their flowing black and brown tresses blew as they hiked up Tzintzuntzan's pyramids shaped like Bundt cakes.

Tzintzuntzan. Can you say it? Tzintzuntzan. It's not as hard to say as Parangaricutirimícuaro. Parangaricutirimícuaro is near the ruins of Tzintzuntzan, but its ruins are crispier. Some of them are still under the volcano that Pompeii'd all over it.

Verbal archeologists suspect that Tzintzuntzan is onomatopoeic. Guess what it's the sound of. Picture a hummingbird twerking. The sounds accompanying those sharp movements would be *tzin, tzun,* and *tzan.*

My lover and I lived in our own Tzintzuntzan, a roundish five-floor apartment building where the elevator would discriminate against us for being lesbians, refusing to open for us, and we'd have to hike the stone stairs to our lair. Hummingbirds never visited our Astroturf-lined balcony. Instead, pigeons flocked to it. Pigeon couples and threesomes canoodled on top of the air conditioner. Their claws scratched nasty bird sex rhythms into the rust. One psycho pigeon dove into the heating system through the roof and got stuck in a tube. She made dying pigeon sounds until she quieted.

We left that sexual drama downtown when we moved into our blue house. Starlings nest in its red tile roof. Raw peach babies screech for worms while moms sail overhead, on their way to forage in urban playgrounds and Cambodian refugees' vegetable gardens. Brown feathers flutter and fall on our limestone porch. Chunklets of nest fall, too. Bits of down drizzle the century plant that blossoms into a bigger and bigger green star by our front steps.

Hummingbirds drop in for breakfast. I was watching one hovering inches above the dirt. His beak dipped into a Mexican sage's purple inflorescence. My stomach growled. I was in the mood for Mexican food, too. Chorizo. I wanted chorizo but not a man's.

I bent over and reached for our newspaper. I subscribe purely for the crossword puzzle. The hummingbird turned his head and made tiny eye contact. He darted towards our tallest tree, our guayaba, and sailed over its green heights, speeding down the street, over tagged apartments and double-parked cars flashing hazard lights. Pit bulls nobody is interested in spaying or neutering lounged in yards and driveways, waiting to be fed a baby of any race.

I smiled. I knew I'd hear tzintzuntzan again. The buffet I planted attracts both bitchy and easygoing hummingbirds. They enjoy my sage, fremontodendron, and lavender but they will shank you, just like some of the passionate locals, if you stand in the way of the guayaba's ultra-seductive nectar.

Next door to us grows Don Patricio's house. People call me short but I'm tall enough to look down on the part in Don Patricio's hair. My skin color is beige-ish whereas Don Patricio is bronze. His eyelids blink open and shut over double Lake Pátzcuaros. Some assholes think Mexicans with blue eyes don't exist but we are very real. Our eyes can be any color. Even pink. Albinism doesn't care if you're brown.

You can tell from Don Patricio's iron pompadour that he was probably into gyrating like Elvis back in the day. He's hunchbacked and wears one extremely thick-soled shoe so that he won't be a leaning Tower of Pisa. He was putting his thicker sole forward, limping up our driveway the evening my lover and I started unloading moving boxes from our truck. Joining me under guayaba leaves, we shook hands. Pink sunset behind evoked Johnny Appleseed. Don Patricio was being neighborly, warning me about our cul-de-sac's dangers.

"Look!" he said in Spanish. He lifted his cane and pointed its rubber tip at a Trans-Am peeling rubber. The tires blew a gust that lifted and swirled hot pink bougainvillea petals out of the gutter. Lipstick kisses on a window. "Kids live here!" Don Patricio exclaimed. " 'Kids live here,' I've told them but they don't listen! Look! They keep driving forty, fifty, sixty miles per hour up our little street!

"You know, several years ago, a little girl was playing right over there and *TZAN!* a car hit her. She went running up the street without her eye. It was on the headlight. That little girl still lives around her. You'll see her. She's the one without the eye."

I nodded.

"The woman you're with," said Don Patricio, "is she your mother?"

"No," I answered. "She's my partner. We're a couple."

"That's okay," he said. He grinned. Crooked headstones knocked together in his mouth.

Hours later, stacking boxes in our garage, I found a scrapbook leaning against some empty paint cans. I set it down on two of them and opened it. Inside were snapshots of a black lady and a white lady wearing matching rainbow boas and riding matching Harleys among a herd of dykes on bikes. Paging deeper into the scrapbook, I found Melissa Etheridge concert ticket stubs and sobriety chips. I flipped through a bunch of empty pages and arrived at a glossy but wrinkled picture of black boy with a birthday hat strapped on. He was leaning over a table, blowing out seven candles jammed into a chocolate-frosted cake. The black and white dykes were standing on either side of him, wearing party hats and clapping. I recognized our dining room.

I shut the scrapbook. Melancholic but thankful, I set it back in the corner. Pioneers had already accustomed Don Patricio to the lifestyle.

My lover was sitting at our dining room table, crunching on potato chips. She was telling me what had been going on in our tree when she'd pulled into our driveway that noon.

"I saw his feet first," she said.

"The crooked shoes?" I asked.

"Yes! I don't even know how he got into the tree with his legs that way," I said. "Maybe he has wings. He does have that hump." I paused to imagine Don Patricio's wings.

My lover continued, "He was just sitting in the branches like it was normal. Eating. And when I got out of the car, he goes, 'Hello neighbor.' " She did her best to imitate his Mexican accent. " 'Just enjoying the weather. And the fruit.' " She mimicked him holding out a guayaba.

"What did you do?"

"Nothing."

"Maybe that's his thing. Climbing lesbians' trees and eating their fruit."

"What should I do if he does it again?"

"Let him, I guess. It must be his lifestyle."

Neighbors don't give a shit about the gorgeous succulents and cacti I've planted along our driveway. All they care about is the guayaba tree that came with our house.

On their way to the bus stop, neighbors stop at our white gate and stare at it. Their lips move so that you can tell their mouths are watering. In Spanish, they tell me, "Your tree, it's giving a lot of fruit this year."

"Yes," I agree, glad that I'm carrying my machete. I will protect my succulents and cacti. They will not be trampled by raza lusting after my fruit.

Handle digs into my forearm, and I reach into my jungle, harvesting. I don't even have to pull the guayabas. All I have to do is graze them. Touching them loosens them and *tzun!* they fall into my orange bucket.

It gets too heavy to handle. The weight is strangling the circulation in my hand so I reach under the bucket, hold it with both hands, and step down from the wooden chair I had dragged out here, back into the dirt. I don't care that the bucket is just half full. These are some heavy-ass fruits.

I scurry down our driveway, turn left, and hoof along the nopales doing jazz hands under Don Patricio's windows. When their paddles have been macheted off and bloody green stumps bleed, I know someone over there is eating her fiber.

I head up Don Patricio's driveway, stepping on bricks that match for a little while and then some new bricks that match for a little while, and then some different bricks that match for another little while. An armless plaster cherub grins in front of a sliding glass door. A Pekingese runs out. Goo crusts the corners of his eyes, and his nails clack against the clashing bricks. The animal yaps at my ankles, and my flip-flops make obscene slurping noises as he follows me up the front steps. I set the bucket down between my ankles. I call, "Hello!" My knuckles rap the screen door's metal frame.

The screen shoves open. A man looks down his goatee at me. He smiles, screams, "Chela!" paces to a corner couch, and plops down.

The TV shouts, "Gol!"

Like a nosy bird, I peak into Don Patricio's. The tile floor shines. Greens coat the walls. Traditional Mexican furniture — equipales and reed stuff — mix with particleboard hutches and shelves. Extra walls suggest compartments. Don Patricio's home is a hive. A honeycomb. How many generations of bees live here?

A brown-haired woman wearing glasses, her hands dripping water, hurries across the tile to greet me.

"Hi," I tell her. "I'm your neighbor to the back."

"Oh, so you're the one who moved in! Nice to meet you!"

Wondering what Don Patricio might've said about me, I blush. "Here," I say, pointing. "I brought guayabas."

"Wow," she says. "We love guayabas. How did you know?" I look at her like *Are you serious?*

"Pato!" she screams. "Pato!" A barefoot boy wearing mesh shorts and a soccer jersey scampers forth from one of the compartments.

"M'ijo," says Chela, "take the guayabas to the kitchen and wash them so that we can give the lady back her bucket."

"Oh, that's okay," I say. "I don't need the bucket right now. When you're done, just leave it by the gate."

"Wow, thank you!" She grins.

"No problem," I say and turn, waving over my shoulder. I hurry past the cherub that can't hug me.

Guayabas are strafing our driveway. Horseflies are pigging out on their explosions. It's necrophilically erotic. The yellow fruits crack open in a sexy and explicit way. Like autopsies, their cotton candy pink cores turned inside out and glistening. Their odor delights flies, ants, cockroaches, and Mexicans. I cannot spell Mexican with Me.

I spend September peeling splattered guayaba grenades off the driveway and chucking them into my cactus garden. The pretty dead feed my prickly living. Heat cooks some of the guayabas. Carbs bind these to the cement. I pick at them with my hoe till they crack loose and crumble.

The guayaba tree is trying to touch its knees with its branches but our car is getting in the way and the guayaba won't give up. It scratches the paint. When you get out on the passenger side, you are in the forest. I skip to the garage, fish my machete out of my red toolbox, and skip back to the tree. I hack my tool against a young branch, and it's left holding on by almost nothing. With my hand, I yank on the mutilation. It comes off like that.

A hummingbird bursts out of the leaves. He tzintzuntzans around my head. His tiny pissed off eyes glare at me. He twerks close enough to sit on my blade.

I keep hacking and yanking. He swirls like an atomic diagram around my head.

I grip the trunk and keep hacking. Ants parade from gray bark to my hand. Their march tickles. Theirs mouths sting. I pause, slap a few of them dead, and shake off their carcasses. I resume my hatchet job. Sawdust trickles. My nostrils suck some in and the urge to sneeze dances in my loins.

A dark toothpick tries to stab my eyeball. The hummingbird thinks I'm a pincushion or something. I wave my machete in his face.

"Leave me alone," I say. "Beat it!"

Blurry wings lift the fighter backwards and high. He exits the jungle. Silhouetted against the sky, he looks at me one more time and flies away.

I keep chopping. Falling branches create a rainforest floor. The bigger branches need extra hacking. I skip to the garage and trade my machete for a saw. With this tool dangling from my forearm, I wheel the trashcan to my mess.

I flip open the lid. I heave and set a thick branch across the maw. I chop. As I dismember, twigs fall. They're tinder.

Tzin. I look up. Black needle comes at my cheek.

"I told you to go away," I say, but foreboding wrinkles my soul. My saw clatters to the driveway. I lift the branch I'm in the process of annihilating. A nest that could host three Jordan almonds is fashioned to the bark.

"Oh no," I mutter.

Tzin, insists the hummingbird. *See? Do you see? Do you see what you've done?*

I trot up our front steps and burst inside. My lover is sitting cross-legged on our baby blue couch, lost in her laptop. I say, "Hey."

"What?"

"I just chopped down a hummingbird nest. I feel like the apocalypse." My voice cracked at the word "feel". Tears are stinging me, same as they did the time pigeons fucking on our balcony annoyed me and I threw a hairbrush at one. After it bounced off of her, she limped. I couldn't deal with the fact that my impatience had maimed a wild thing. I wanted to jump off the balcony without so much as an abandoned mattress to cushion my fall.

"You have to be more careful out there!" shouts my lover. As she shuts her laptop, I look down at my feet. I see green feet. I'm an ogre. I really need to cut my toenails.

"I know," I mumble.

"Did you touch it?" she asks.

"No," I lie. My index finger grazed it.

"Bring it in here."

I hop outside, fetch the branch, come back, and hold the twig before my lover. She peers at it, examining it.

"Try to reattach it."

"With what?"

"Rope, I guess."

I swish back outside to the garage, and snatch some rope off a shelf. I head back to the scene of the crime. I press the twig flat against a muscular branch and wind rope around both, binding them together. I loop and pull tight three big knots that blend into the wood. I stand back. I try to think of my creation as a tree house, Swiss Hummingbird Family Robinson, but it looks like what it is. Like a human without an engineering degree destroyed something fragile and tried to put it back together. Humpty Dumpty.

Each morning, after my coffee, I scoop the newspaper off the driveway and check out the nest. November rains come. They drench the little home, turning it into a soggy cereal that poops onto the ground. The eggs never hatch but the ground gobbles them up so I guess they mulch my cacti. I watch hummingbirds dart towards anything sweet. They suckle at the sage. They still come to eat Mexican, but they aren't as perky. They treat the guayaba the way Mom and Dad treated Tzintzuntzan, as romantic ruins.

Bird Hair

Life is a Prologue
and then you die.
I hope you enjoyed that
mango pie.

I'm sitting at Abuelita's dining room table, chewing pink tamal. My greedy bitch-ass uncle and the woman he's in the process of making his ex-wife shuffle into the room. They enter with very, very _____ steps. (Sometimes, if there's no adjective to describe something, leave it alone. Wait for someone else to invent the word.) Greedy tío's face works with his wife's. They're Greek chorus masks telling us something is the matter.

In flattened voice, greedy tío announces, "My mother died."

Everyone in the dining room, Mom and Dad and Tío Miguel and Tía Ofelia, get different looks on their faces, but the looks communicate that their feelings are coming from the same place: the spring where horrible feelings come from.

We leave whatever stupid thing we're doing — sipping atole, stirring atole, dipping pastries in this doughy drink, dough, dough, dough dough, dodo birds — and we rise and fly up the tiled hall, past Abuelito's office and into the room where we fed Abuelita apple juice with a dropper and changed her diapers while never commenting on how her ancient pussy hair spilled like a unicorn's beard. Those last weeks we watched her move her hands in front of her mouth, and, you know, it seemed she was pulling invisible stings from it. That's what everyone kept commenting. "Why is she pulling strings? It looks like she's pulling strings from her mouth?"

Isn't that what the Fates did in Greek mythology? Spin, measure, and snip the thread of life? Abuelita's room reeked of the Mexican dying process. The Mexican dying process smells of pulled strings, and pulled strings are the thin soul of a lady who enjoyed painting things far more ordinary and real than Frida Kahlo's lifestyle.

Abuelita was an artist of everyday strings.

Greedy tío and Tío Miguel shuffle around Abuelita's bed, a hungry baby and a good baby. Their lips quiver an orphan quiver that seems extra pathetic in light of their middle age and prostate problems.

Tía Ofelia positions herself to the left of the bed. She shuffles inside herself. Spiritually. Outlined in permanent makeup, her tattooed eyes turn upward toward our heavens, a ceiling fan, and Ofelia's voice invokes, "God!" so hard and painfully that her humanity molts and falls away, useless as feathers. She turns into one of the birds Abuelita used to keep caged in her dining room. Somewhere in the past, Abuelita is shuffling towards a cage, hands outstretched, stale cookie crumbs in her palm.

Ofelia's head bobbles. Now bird, she screeches in tongues we understand. She screeches God's name over and over in undiscovered languages.

I'm trembling not like a leaf but like someone who has never sat at someone's bedside after her heart has set down its weapon. Pulled the final string and let it fall dental-flossily.

The panic attack I'm suffering is happening so mildly it's flying under the radar.

I press my thighs together. I'm wearing gray shorts without underwear, and I don't want anyone to see my pubes. I'm sitting on the bed beside Abuelita's. On this bed, two months ago, Tío Miguel woke up beside Abuelito the day he became a dead Mexican.

Later On

Abuelita's doctor happens to be the asshole's wife. Her manicured hands are winding gauze from the top of Abuelita's head, down her cheek, along her chin, up her other cheek, and repeating this trajectory, framing her face with a white O. The dressing reminds me of Jacob Marley's ghost, but I don't dare share this Dickensian connection with anyone.

Diverticulitis

Tía Ofelia calls the funeral home to arrange for them to come pick up Abuelita's body. She tells them, "No, no, you don't have to come immediately. Wait a few hours." Abuelita's youngest daughter, my Tía Pancha, is wincing in a hospital bed, waiting to have some of her colon scooped out, so she's going to have to sneak out in order to come say goodbye.

This is the AAunt Who Lives for Alcoholics Anonymous, Cigarettes, Fried Food, and Enya's Music. Somehow, She Became Convinced That Enya Committed Suicide in the Name of Love, But Enya Didn't, and Honestly, I Think That's Why Enya's Music Seems So Sweet to Her

Tía Pancha's daughters drive her to Abuelita's. The taller of these two beauties with close-set eyes is standing in front of me. Pre-Colombian masks hanging from a small strip of wall by the spare bedroom appear to listen to us.

"I feel relief," my cousin whispers to me. "Don't you?"

Her eyes, which blur together as one, stare down my conscience. I remember a conversation we had two weeks ago in the dining room. A fly had buzzed as I'd whispered, "Sometimes, when no one is looking, I want to put a pillow over Abuelita's face so that she'll stop suffering."

My cousin's eyes had bulged closer together. "Me, too," she said.

White Sox

"She needs socks," Ofelia is murmuring. "When my daughter died, we had to put socks on her."

Dad, who wears size EEE, disappears from the doorway. He reappears with a pair of socks we could use as a coffin.

"I think I have some that'll fit better," I say. I walk to the bedroom where Abuelito's ghost interrupted me while I was facebooking. My suitcase is plopped onto the desk, and I reach in and grab a pair of white anklets. No one has ever worn them. Abuelita is going to take their virginity. My lover's mom gave them to me as a stocking stuffer.

With giant awareness that I'm bringing socks to my dead grandmother's feet, I carry them to her bed, lean over her body, and pull her white sheet towards her knees. Mom and I lift her swollen foot. I slide white cotton past curled toes and broken blood vessels. Mom holds the leg while my fingers make sure that elastic fits the right way around the ankle. The sock needs to fit right. Abuelita will be wearing it when forever ends.

Family Business

I'm standing by the nosy Pre-Colombian masks again, this time with Pancha's shorter, but still beautiful, daughter.

"We had to smuggle my mom out of the hospital because we haven't paid her bill, yet," she whispers. Grinning in spite of the smell, she adds, "She was contraband!"

Her family, which includes a Colombian sister-in-law, has experience keeping cargo in motion.

Dressing Up

Ofelia and I are crossing the street. We are walking into a women's clothing store named after feminine sin: Vanity.

We stop among metal racks. Ofelia orders, "Find a white blouse."

All the clothes look black or colorful until a flock of white sweaters catches my eye. "White sweaters," I say, pointing.

"My mother was small," Ofelia mumbles. "Find one in small."

We migrate to the white sweaters and flip through them. I say, "I think the littlest is medium."

Ofelia takes the littlest sweater from me, holds it up, and scrutinizes it. We turn to see the asshole and his wife standing among frocks. From her finger, she dangles the white sweater. Ofelia asks them, "What do you think?"

"That's not her," says the asshole. "My mother doesn't wear things like that."

He's right. It's an ugly sweater. It's nerdy and too hot for August. The asshole's frown surveys the store. He points at a lace dress. He says, "What about that beige thing?"

Ofelia steps over to the beige thing, and reaches for its price tag. She reads it. I think about how the dress seems slightly slutty, but since the bottom half of Abuelita's coffin will probably stay shut during her wake, it might be okay. A salesgirl smiles at us. "For whom are you buying this dress?" she asks.

"For our mother," answers Ofelia. "She just died."

The salesgirl's smile runs in our opposite direction.

"Yes, this is the one," says Ofelia. "This is the dress. Do you have it in small?"

The salesgirl nods and walks to the front of the store. She steps into the window display, reaches for the hem, and pulls our requested dress up over the head of a shiny, white mannequin lacking distinct facial features. Draping the dress over her arm, the salesgirl carries it to us. More salesgirls flock to the counter.

"Who are you buying this dress for?" asks a salesgirl with a bony face.

"My mother," answers Ofelia. "She died about an hour ago. She lived in that house over there." Ofelia lifts her hands and points with a finger wearing a ring so gaudy it must be an apology.

The salesgirl's grin falls. It splatters on the floor. She nods, reaches for tissue paper, and sets the dress on it. As she wraps it, the salesgirl cries without making any noise. None of her tears fall on the tissue paper or the dress. Why is she crying? It's not like her abuelita just died.

Photographing the Imaginary

Ofelia sets the dress on the bed where Abuelito's soul stepped out of his body. She leaves me alone with Abuelita's body and the beige dress. I point my camera at the dress, tap the button, and take a picture that is as good as a ghost.

Photographing Things That Tell Time So That They Become Stuck in a Certain Place in Time

I'm taking pictures of everything because when something meaningful dies, everything you look at, whether it does so nicely or cruelly, reminds you of the difference between alive versus its opposite. I say to Ofelia, "I feel like I have to take a picture of everything."

She nods and holds radishes under the kitchen faucet. We are going to eat pozole for dinner. You can't have pozole without radishes.

I snap pictures of the kitchen clock and the microwave clock; it has special buttons for warming tortillas, chilaquiles, and other traditional foods,. I think about poetry that tells time, mostly W.H. Auden's. Auden wasn't Mexican, though, you can take his name and sound out a Mexican state: W-H-aca.

Photographing Virgins

An albondiga of a man and a crow of a man have climbed out of a black van they parked in the driveway. They unlatch metal legs and leave their gurney near the bathroom. The albondiga peers into Abuelita's room. Miguel comments, "You must have a lot of experience handling people's loved ones with delicate care."

The albondiga answers, "Yes, we are always delicate with... people." While he continues reassuring Miguel of his expertise, I think about Miguel's prostrate cancer, which my mind adds an R to, prostrate cancer. I remember how when Ofelia and her daughters picked us up at the airport and drove us to Abuelita's a few weeks ago, Ofelia was gossiping in the backseat about how Miguel's cancer medicine might make him sprout chichis. Looking out the car windows, I saw yellow squares against black. Windows at night. I asked Ofelia, "Isn't it better to have chichis and be alive than the other alternative?" She lit a cigarette, rolled down her window, and changed the subject to whether or not Abuelita might be possessed and should we shop for an exorcist.

The albondiga and the crow stand at the foot of Abuelita's bed, staring at her death, listening to Miguel who is still talking. He's always talking. He's dead right now but he's still talking. I'm sitting on the wood and twine chair beside Abuelita. A headshot of the Virgin of Guadalupe hangs from the white wall above us. She Mona-Lisa gazes upon both of us. I have finally put on calzones. Dad looks through his camera lens and snaps a photo of Abuelita, the Virgin, and me. He leaves out the crow, the albondiga, and Miguel.

Photographing People Being Grief-Stricken Weirdoes

As we'd screamed and wept and invoked God as a family right after Abuelita quit pulling strings, the asshole had gone and fetched his camera, too. He'd gotten to work taking pictures of our spectacle.

Somebody always takes the pictures while somebody else makes the spectacle, and if they're alive, Abuelitas paint pictures of what's happening and sing and feed the birds.

Photographing Colombians

I'd found out through email that one of my friends had died two days before Abuelita. This friend, a Colombian Sappho — una poetisa increíblemente lésbica — had told me a story that helped me understand that my family was less sick than I felt we were for documenting Abuelita's dead body and our reactions to it.

My friend had confessed to me that once in Bogotá at an aunt's funeral, she'd watched a cemetery worker jimmy open a dank mausoleum in order to rearrange the caskets. He was preparing to accommodate the woman sleeping in the coffin near everyone's feet, but the man's grip on a casket holding a long-dead aunt turned to margarine. Her box plummeted, hit brick, and crashed open. Pieces of long-dead aunt and beetles puffed and drizzled everywhere, a morbid pepper, and I asked her, "What did you do?"

In an unfazed voice, she replied, "I got out my phone and started doing this." She motioned taking pictures.

Who Gives Birds Haircuts?

Ofelia and I are driving to the flower stands across the street from the cemetery. We buy an arrangement composed of palm fronds and white roses, nestle it in the backseat, and drive to the funeral home. We go to the showroom and choose a coffin, and slide Abuelita's birth certificate and a rosary across the undertaker's desk. Ofelia tells the undertaker, "Put the rosary in her hands." The undertaker nods. Her lipstick is unflattering.

Ofelia and I stand in the pretty much empty mortuary parlor where the wake will happen. We watch a guy unlock Abuelita's casket, pull back the wooden lid, and — no lie, no exaggeration — Abuelita looks drop dead deathly gorgeous and relaxed. Dying totally Botoxed her forehead. Ofelia leaves to go take care of more business, there's so much bureaucracy when you die, and I spend time alone with Abuelita, gazing at her through a pane of glass that is the window to her face. I admire her cartilage and cheekbones so miraculous that they died for our sins. Once the wake gets underway and professors and gastroenterologists and businessmen and AAunts arrive to hug, kneel, pray, take pictures, eat cookies, and sip coffee, I wander to the rear of the funeral home, to a patio even the moonlight is afraid of, where birdcages big enough to be buried in stand in the four corners. Certain sections of me are always on the patio, in that special darkness, hanging out with the birds that have the strangest little haircuts. Haircuts like Buddhist dykes.

Even This Title Is a Ghost

Ghosts don't need anybody to believe in them. They just are. Like pimples, autism, and steam. My dad's dad, who was and will be my only American grandfather ever, didn't believe in ghosts. He believed in beer, and he believed in eating people's house pets. He traveled to México during the Great Depression, which is México always, and he was wandering through a forest filled with owls, which were actually shape-shifting brujas, witches, when he heard somebody singing a pretty and sad song.

My grandfather tiptoed to the owly forest's edge and peaked around a needly tree trunk. He spied a village's outskirts and on these outskirts was the thing you want outside your skirt, a cemetery. (This village, its outskirt, and the forest exist only in the story I'm telling. Sundown was upon them.)

Grandpa leaned on the tree's hip, watching Mexicans. It seemed that all the Mexicans who lived in this village were congregating there in their graveyard, which is creepy. Very goth. Muy goth. Which Mexicans can't say. The *th* sound escapes them. They got goth. Got goth?

The singing that drew Grandpa was coming from a big-ass biscuit of a minstrel whose bloatedness was straining his white shirt and pants almost too much. The guitar he was playing seemed a toy thanks to his William Howard Taftness. His mustache and moist, moist chin were parting and wagging while he crooned a tragic melody about a black dove. The song was so sad that it didn't verge on ridiculous, it was ridiculous, and it was so ridiculous that it was a tragedy, and it was such a tragedy that it was ridiculous, and I could go on like this for the rest of the story, but then you might want me to die, and I enjoy living too much.

Billows of baby's breath cushioned the earth between graves, creating a flower fog, and marigolds bunches dotted the fog hither and hither, and each headstone had been transformed into an altar honoring the likes, and not the dislikes, of that particular dead villager.

Flower wreathes woven together with ribbons were hanging from tombstones, and pictures of the dead and little trinkets that must've meant something to them when they were breathersa pet rock here, a tube of half-used lipstick there, a blunt here, a negligee therewere draped from the wreathes or arranged just beneath them. Also, at these gravesite altars, foods breathed odors and heat. Bowls of pozole were stabbed with spoons, and womanly papayas were chopped into wet and ready halves, and piles of guayabas smelled of ripe jock strap, and there was even a roasted rabbit with a mini-mango shoved in its mouth and gooseberry eyes making it a representative of Satan.

There milled a few women dressed like great ladies, with hair wound into high buns, but most of the women praying rosaries at the graves were hobbity peasants who knew more about plows and standing child birth than those light-skinned bitches. These darker women embraced the rainbow and it embraced them: they wore its colors woven through their blouses, skirts, shawls, and ribbons streaming along their braids. The cemetery men wore white unless they were the bitchy snobs' husbands. The bitchy snobs' husbands wore charcoal-colored three-piece suits and mild grimaces.

A priest was dawdling at a grave. Its head stone was chiseled with the name Jesús de Jesús. He was wearing a black shirt and black trousers. The small white stain near his crotch represented…innocence.

Curious about what was up, Grandpa let go of his tree. He walked up to an ageless Mexican kneeling in dirt, playing with a cricket. His cricket appeared trained to respond to his hand signals and hopped to the right when the man snapped his right hand. The cricket hopped to the left when the man snapped his left hand. In fact, the man looked a bit like the cricket, but this is not unusual. Human and pet often come to resemble one another as do husband and wife, master and slave, and babysitter and babysittee.

In New Jersily-accented Spanish, Grandpa pleaded, "Excuse me." The man and the cricket stopped their game and looked up. Grandpa asked, "What's going on?" He gestured at the ado. "Why aren't the people eating the food?"

The Mexican bent his right hand, lowered it, and the cricket hopped on for the ride. The cricket man took a luxurious amount of time standing up, and once he was erect, he petted his insect.

"Tonight," the guy explained, "after all these living people have gone back to their big or little houses, they will go to sleep. When they are asleep, and deep in the place where dreams happen, the spirits of the dead will crawl through a funny keyhole that only turns tonight. When these visitors come, believe me, they're hungry."

Grandpa's smirk told the cricket stroker all he needed to hear.

The cricket man and his bug stared him down. "Stay," the guy challenged. It was apparent from the cricket's stare that it was challenging him, too. "You'll see."

Wanting to prove the bug man a pendejo, Grandpa decided to stay. As the sky turned black, black, black, black, black, the Tafty guitarist quit strumming. Women rounded up their cheeky kids. Old ladies lifted their fingers to bless themselves with the sign of the cross and then ran these same fingers along their goatees. Young and youngish women pulled their shawls tightly around their chichis. Nobody likes a chilly chichi.

A breeze stirred marigolds, fallen pine needles, and tissue paper decorations strung from tomb to tomb. These featured precisely cut flowers or skulls and skeletons in action, riding horses and playing cards. These images reminded everybody that they'd better get home and get in bed and quit looking delicious: The dead were coming to town and they were bringing mortal appetites.

Families, orphans, lovers, and the priest emptied out of the cemetery and flowed down various roads. Talented brats sucked their fists and snorted, and a doe watched from a bramble thicket, glad that her immediate family wasn't in any of the tamales in the graveyard. Those were beef, pork, possum, and stray puppy. The doe turned her pretty butt and pranced into the owl/witch pine forest.

Mexicans abandoned Grandpa with his fear, which was small, an ember. Grandpa wadded his poncho and wedged it between a headstone and earth. He rested his platinum hair and giant Slavic forehead on it. Candles on a nearby tequila baron's tomb flickered. Wax dripped. Flames gave up and joined the dead. Grandpa wanted to keep vigil but his blonde eyelashes were a bitch. They got in they way. Mexico blackened. He snored.

Gluttonous sounds were crawling into his ears, and it wasn't a trick. He smelled the flowers and remembered those were for the dead, and his fingertips scratched against the tombstone he was hugging. He remembered, "I'm in Mexico, I'm in a cemetery, and I'm here to prove that that Mexican with the cricket is a fool."

His heart was beating faster than my hamster's in the seconds before she was murdered, but Grandpa didn't want to die lying down so he knelt and snaked his face up along the letters D-E-P, the Hispanic world's equivalent of R-I-P. He peeked across initials. His breath stopped as his blue eyes adjusted to darkness interrupted by the glow of a few tenacious votive candles. He saw them.

One was shoving his tongue down a cognac glass and lapping brandy. Two were tearing a tortilla into snowflakes. One was chewing an unwrapped tamal, and her neighbor was chomping the soft, good part out of a bolillo and leaving the crust like the trash it is. One was belching and hadn't developed a language to apologize with, and one was biting, BITING another's pink nalgas. The one being bitten squealed and dropped her macaroon. The bully swooped in and snatched the fallen food, scarfing it.

Three little pigs times three little pigs times three little pigs equals many more pigs. These pigs weren't in shape enough to be wild. Their cellulite, blonde hair, and complexions gave away their domesticity. They were somebody's. A herd of future lunches and breakfasts.
Grandpa's fear melted like nuked Velveeta.

He watched the pigs tear it up and party till the earth's rotation lightened the night. Sky grayed, and then came a greenish tint, like when sewer gas casts a romantic haze over the ghetto. This evil color is particularly pretty when it appears in the human iris. The pigs glanced at the horizon and took the changing sky as a warning. They lifted their snouts and turned their butts to their mess. Ears bounced, ears that would've been delicious fried, as they trotted away. They must've been headed back to the pens they'd escaped from. They must've been looking forward to sleeping off their crudas. Los hangovers. Hangover de puerquito. Oink-oink, barf-barf, oink, barf, dream.

Something was wagging Grandpa's foot. He opened his eyes and saw sun backlighting a human form.

"Gringo!" the form boomed. "Hi!"

Grandpa sat up. Monarch butterflies tangled in the lovemaking act humped past. The human form leaned left. Now Grandpa could see him. It was the cricket stroker.

"What did I tell you?" he asked. "Look! The food is gone!" The cricket stroker puckered his lower lip at the graveyard mess. Since he was missing his front bottom teeth, his chin crumpled inward.

Grandpa smiled. He felt proud that he had the ultimate *neiner neiner neiner* to toss at the fool. "There aren't any spirits!" Grandpa cried. "Pigs came to eat the food! I saw them! They came and ate your offerings! Your ghosts are *bacon*."

The cricket stroker shrugged, smiled, and asked, "Can't chorizo and a memory of something you loved be the same thing?"

My grandpa realized, *the man's cricket… was gone.*

Be Hoof, Behave, Behoove (and Be Hooves): A Four-Legged Triptych
Featuring Pigs Both Chauvinist and Piloncillo

I. Be Hoof

Los cochinitos ya están en la cama
muchos besitos les dió su mamá
y calientitos todos con pijama
dentro de un rato los tres roncarán…

Between the Sunday morning that she stopped moving her hands as if
pulling invisible strings from her mouth and the early Tuesday evening that
is this sentence, three people have lain in the place where Abuelita lived her
last five years, what looks like an anemic bed.

Tío Rafael, a "used car salesman" who flew in from Tijuana, slept in it
after her wake. I worried his girth was going to break it. The bed survived.
It must be very strong.

Walking past Abuelita's bedroom door some hours ago, I glimpsed my
asshole tío lying on her bed, staring at the ceiling fan. It was clear that he
was thinking. Probably about how sad it is that he's an orphan now and
what kind of poison he should use to kill his wife.

Now I have the bed to myself. Everyone else has left to attend the first
in a trio of nighttime masses that will be held for Abuelita's soul, to help it
get to where it should be, which isn't here. I'm not kneeling with the rest of
my family, pretending to pray, sitting out holy communion, because after
we watched four gravediggers in mom jeans and long-sleeved t-shirts lift
Abuelita's casket by rope, lower it onto Abuelito's, shovel dirt over it, nestle
bricks over the dirt, spread mortar over the bricks, shovel more dirt on
top, watch us fling white roses down the hole, shovel the last of the dirt on
top, and plop my great-grandparents' graham cracker of a headstone over
the mound (they're somewhere in that plot, too), all dusty we drove to a
restaurant by that roundabout where a big-ass statue of Minerva holds a

spear that could shish-kabob rhinos.

Ofelia's husband, Tío Ramon, called the owner ahead of our arrival so that when we entered through the restaurant's back door, a black taffeta bow hung over heads. A hostess led us to three tables pushed together. Our grief attracted mariachis with womanly thighs. They clustered around our emotions. Miguel creaked out of his seat to join them in song. "Llorar y Llorar!" he insisted. He screamed and wept through the ranchera. His skinny voice drowned the fat voice of the square-faced mariachi, "...cry and cry, it's useless now that I've lost you! I want you back! Come save me, wake me, rescue me from this suffering..."

Tears wept down Miguel's Miguel Hidalgo face. Got stuck in the creases leading to his lips. Never exited these canyons. In English, the lyrics of "Llorar y Llorar" sound melodramatic. In Spanish, they sound patriotic. Histrionics fuel Mexican-ness.

Fountain gargling in the patio behind me teased my bladder. My eyes wandered after a rogue mariachi straying towards purple geraniums. He lifted his leg and planted boot heel against flower planter. Bow poked out of his back pocket. Violin lackadaisically dangled from his left hand. From the lap of his skintight pants, he slid a phone. Flipped it open. Fingered a text. I love it when mariachis text. It's like watching tradition text.

As the other mariachis strummed, growled, and blew, and my asshole uncle rose to out sing Miguel, I turned to examine the items on the terracotta tray a waitress was sliding before me. I grimaced. I pointed and asked, "What's that?"

My cousin laughed at me. "A pig's foot," she answered.

I didn't need to say "gross." My American bitch face said it.

She laughed. "You've never eaten foot before?" she asked.

"No. I've never had hoof."

"Try it. Come on."

I reached for the foot. Its sliminess felt chilly but not cold. Were we shaking hands?

My other cousin instructed, "Eat it. Eat the foot."

To show them what I'm made of, that my DNA is as sick and earthen as theirs, I slid the foot between my front teeth and nibbled the tip. I imagined

I was chewing my fingernails, and it felt like that, like gnawing cuticle skin. I reached for my coffee cup, brought it to my bitch face, and chased the pork with bitterness. Caffeinated claw.

The foot had tasted so unpedicured. Barnyard. It began bucking this morning. Momentarily, its squirms, quivering. My stomach wants to go for a walk.

Hoof is my wandering companion. The thing that calls us is Abuelita's bed. We go and lie in it. With unkosher thing tracing my stomach lining, I see what Abuelita saw everyday for the last five years. Ceiling fan.

There is a sensation of her hereness and his hereness, and their teasing each other and a shawl. Abuelita never wrote stupid poetry like he did. She sewed clothes. She made living and dead babies. She also made kindness.

She was a vessel but she was everything in her vessel, too. Perfections and imperfections and wrinkles and veins overflowed from her. She could be mean sometimes. Once when my brother annoyed her, she grabbed him by the elbow, dragged him to Abuelito's study, shoved him in there, and locked the door. A legit punishment. There was no TV in there. Only books, lust, and dust.

A white string dangles from the ceiling fan. My hands float to my mouth and pull invisible string from my throat. This string unfurls from an infinite spool that winds inside me and you, and connects us to every important work of art.

I look across my ribs and see my feet curled at the foot of her bed. I slid socks identical to the ones I'm wearing over Abuelita's bare feet while they were warmish but stiffening, becoming hooves. I think about moving my big toe. Decide not to.

Some piece of linen smells of her life and death. These yin and yang scents are something you can't and don't necessarily want to rinse away. There's something horribly cathartic in their coexistence. Yin and yang. Hoof and mouth.

II. Behave

Los cochinitos ya están en la cama
muchos besitos les dió su mamá
y calientitos todos con pijama
dentro de un rato los tres roncarán

Uno soñaba que era rey
y de momento quiso un pastel
su gran ministro hizo traer
500 paseteles nomás para el...

Sun has set behind the ice cream parlor, the pharmacy, the Center for the Study of Down Syndrome, the chiropractor's office, the ladies clothing store where we bought Abuelita's last dress, and moldy square homes guarded by metallic gates.

Shoulders hunch below light bulb flickering over dining room table. Being in Abuelita's bed after dark hadn't felt right. Once darkness overpowered, it felt as if she was still in the bed, pulling strings. The hoof and I retreated.

I stare at the chocolatey piano by the sliding glass door. I once heard Abuelita and her oldest sister, Caridad, exchange words over a piano. I don't know if this is the one that inspired their tête-à-tête.

"That's mine," Abuelita had accused, pointing at the piano in Caridad's living room.

With dentures coated with burnt gelatina, which is pig bone ground into dessert, Caridad argued, "It wouldn't still be in the family if it wasn't for me." She lifted her lipstick-stained napkin to her mouth and made it even more feminine. As she daubed, her frizzy curls didn't move.

My plate of burnt gelatina clicked as I set in on the table. My butt cheeks tensed. I was ready to watch two old broads duke it out.

"That doesn't matter!" cried Abuelita. "My father gave me that piano as a wedding gift! You and your husband KIDNAPPED IT!"

"That's because your irresponsible husband would have sold it!

That was one of the few things our father gave us when we lived in the orphanage!"

"THAT DOESN'T MATTER! My father told me *I* could have that piano. *You* and *your husband* kidnapped it on my WEDDING NIGHT."

Under gelatina breath, Caridad whispered, "Which wasn't the night you got pregnant."

Rage atrophied Abuelita's lower lip. It quivered.

Instead of comforting her, I rose. I faked intestinal distress.

"Excuse me," I said. "My gelatina is in a hurry."

I had turned fifteen two months prior and was, according to this birthright, a full-blown woman. My parents had gifted me a birthday trip to Guadalajara where I would stay with different relatives and go deep into my Mexicanity. Mom and Dad had talked to me about issues like how to avoid being kidnapped and never asking a policeman for help, but they had not coached me about how to deal with hearing an abuelita called a slut. They had not coached me about how to deal with an abuelita's tears. Nothing inside me knew what to do about a wounded abuelita. Seeing an abuelita cry and being unable to comfort her made me certain I wasn't really a woman. I was still becoming one. Hardening into one. Hardening into that kind of seed.

Unsure of where Caridad's toilet was, I wandered hallways. Humidity was yanking their wallpaper free. Long silky folds drooped and reached for tile floor, undressing the plaster. Water damage stained it yellowish and rusty, like urine was seeping through the walls. They were stained that color and gave off that smell, but it must've been plain water, the water that surprises you everywhere in Guadalajara, in the air, your hair, your mouth, the sewers, the jicama, your skin, the gutters, and the clouds.

Peering into each room I passed, I saw evidence that supported Dad's accusation that Caridad was a hoarder. Sneering rocking horses wearing cobweb veils. Hand-painted wardrobes bursting with wedding dresses, christening gowns, and bathrobes. Statues of bearded and tonsured saints without hands and feet. A crib fit for Rosemary's heavy baby. Empty birdcages and empty birdcages and empty birdcages and empty birdcages and empty birdcages. A lace parasol whose original color could've been anything. Louis XIV style armchairs. Mirrors, mirrors, mirrors. A room jammed with grandfather clocks.

Occasional squeals from the piano war found me. The hall dead-ended in a bathroom. Leaning against the doorway of the room before the john, I saw pelt draping the back of a rocking chair.

"Nacho..." I whispered.

Dad had once told me that the love of Caridad's life wasn't her husband, a peanut magnate named Pánfilo, but a cocker spaniel named after a chip. Caridad's maid modified their love affair when she left the front door open. Realizing her mistake, the maid marched outside to see if Nacho had gotten out and of course he had. A bus had hit him but only knocked the life out of him. He had retained his canine shape. He hadn't exploded and rained like an over-the-hill tomato hitting the dirt.

"Senora!" cried the maid. "Nacho!"

Caridad sprinted into the street, scooped dog corpse into her arms, and drove it to a man whose art relied on death. The man fashioned Nacho into décor Caridad could still stroke. A little rug. A pelt. The spaces where he'd had eyeballs puckered with emptiness.

I wanted to touch him as badly as I'd wanted to touch my murdered cousin in his coffin. Tiptoeing into his room, I stood by his chair. The room's disuse stank very particularly. Nacho's blindness stared at me. So did the maid. She was looking at me in the way that ghosts stare. Both were waiting for me to say something, something that would acknowledge their continued presence.

I wondered if Nacho licked the hands of the spirits that stayed in the house.

Dad had told me about one. He had lived with Caridad, Pánfilo, and their daughters when he was in twenties, and Caridad gave him a room in her hallway of spares. She fed Dad, too. Helped him practice his half-Mexican Spanish.

Dad worked teaching English and music at a private school. One day, he came home to find his belongings mildly rearranged. He thought a servant might've done it. Forgot about the subtle weirdness.

Next day, when he came back from teaching, instead of being mildly rearranged, Dad found his belongings moderately rearranged. A guitar that had stood in one corner was standing in the corner diagonally across from its home base. An army jacket that had been hanging in the closet had been tossed to the floor. A brown blanket had been pulled from the bed and draped over desk and its chair, as if children were playing fort. The alarm clock told time two hours too fast.

Dad stomped around the house, looking for Caridad. He found her on the living room sofa, stroking Nacho's remains.

He said, "I think your daughters are playing with my stuff when I'm out. Can you tell them to stop?"

Caridad looked up from her love. "Why would they do that?" she asked.

"I don't know," he answered.

"I'll talk to them," she said.

Next day, Caridad told Dad, "I talked to your cousins. They didn't touch your stuff. I don't know who did."

Dad furrowed his billboard forehead.

"If you're so worried about it, get a lock for the door," she advised.

Dad walked to a hardware store, bought a lock, and installed it. His stuff remained undisturbed for three months. On the fourth month, Mom fell in lust with his long hair. *She* came to the house and delivered a bouquet to *him*. Feminism.

After work one evening, Dad slid his key into his extra lock. Turned it. Opened his door. Stepped into a brand new level of chaos. His crap was everywhere. His sheets and blankets had been stripped from his bed and flung at the four corners of his room. The closet doors, dresser drawers, and desk drawers hung in various states ranging from kind of ajar to flung the fuck open, their contents scrambled. Dad's guitar lay on his flat bare mattress. Two snipped strings curled and claw marks scratched along the lacquer.

Dad stormed off, in search of Caridad. This time, he found her in the kitchen, burning something. Her daughters were chopping chayotes on a pine cutting board. A cauldron filled with water burbled on the stove.

"Yes?" asked Caridad.

149

"Somebody came into my room, opened everything, and threw it on the floor! Somebody snipped my guitar strings and scratched it!"

Caridad stared at him. The girls slowed their chopping. Knives went still.

Caridad tapped a wooden spoon against the cauldron's lip. She asked, "Have you considered that maybe it's not a person who's doing this?"

Dad's moustache curled.

Caridad said, "It could be something else."

Caridad's pretty daughter (the assessment is subjective) whispered something to her prettier daughter (even more subjective). The prettier daughter looked at Dad and said, "There's a lady who works by the cathedral who can tell you if it's human or something else. Do you want us to take you to see her?"

Caridad answered, "Yes," for everyone.

Instead of finishing the dinner, Dad, Caridad, and the subjectively pretty and prettier daughters rode in a Pontiac to an apartment building where the special lady they'd discussed lived and received her clientele. She worked at a bitty, round, purple felt-covered table in her living room. As Dad sat across from her, smoothing his hippie combover, Caridad hissed, "*Tell her.*"

"I'm staying with my aunt," Dad explained, gesturing at Caridad. "It started so slowly I thought it was them." He pointed at his cousins, who huddled near a fringed lampshade. "First, I noticed that a few things would get moved around my room while I was away at work. Like a pencil or a sweater would be in a place I knew I hadn't left it. Then bigger things started moving, like my guitar. Then, just, everything. It went for everything."

"Everything?"

"Yes. It likes chaos."

The special lady smiled and asked, "May I hold the ring that was your father's?"

She pointed at the jewelry Dad wore on his right hand. He'd received it after his mom, Grandma B, went to check on Grandpa. He was tinkering in the suburban driveway after Thanksgiving dinner, and Grandpa had enjoyed his food so much that it was killing him. Grandma B watched as Grandpa's shoes and pants, poking out from under the Studebaker's front bumper, started to writhe. Wrench clattered against concrete, like punctuation. Period. The heart attack was finished as paramedics pulled up to the curb. Grandpa stiffened extra fast, marbleizing thanks to all the cholesterol.

Dad slid off the ring and handed it across the felt. He asked, "How did you know it was my father's?"

The special lady took the ring, squeezed it, and explained, "I know the same way that I know that it is not these girls who are rearranging your belongings." As she gestured at the sisters, they huddled closer so that their ears touched. "Neither are the servants. I know who it is." She leaned across the table, closer to Dad's facial hair forest. "Do you want to know who it is?"

Dad froze. Caridad cried out, "Yes!"

With her free hand, the special lady gestured, *Pay me.*

Caridad reached into her purse, pulled out a wad of paper money, coins, lint, stray hairs, and peanut shells. She placed the entity on the table. She whispered to Dad, "You're welcome."

The special lady stared at the wad, shrugged, and began, "The thing that is moving your things is a spirit that belongs to a man who used to live in your aunt's house. His religion was bachelorhood, and he realized his mistake in his old age, but by then, well, the lifestyle was irredeemable. An affliction. He withered away alone, a miser. Since he knew he was going to watch the light die without anyone to pat his hand, he did. He left this world without leaving his fortune to any creature. It remains hidden on your aunt's property, in the ground, with no one to claim it. This man's spirit likes that you're in his house. He likes that there is a young, musical gringo in love. He likes that he has somebody son-like to watch over. He feels like a father towards you as much as a ghost who never had children can. In his dead way, he loves you. He thinks you're a decent person, and he's unaccustomed to decent people." Caridad raised her eyebrows.

"He knows that your girlfriend will ask you to marry her and that you're going to be a good husband and that you'll have three children who you will raise in the United States. You'll take your Mexican wife up there just like your father took his Mexican wife up there. The spirit would like to help you. If you wait in your room tonight, he will come to your door. He will knock. Let the bachelor in and let him sit on your unmade bed. He will tell you where to find his fortune, but you have to be curious enough to let the damned, the forsaken, and the lonely in."

One dead father was enough for Dad. He moved out that night.

I telepathied, "This might've been my dad's room," to Nacho's fur. My fingers itched for his empty eye sockets. To get rid of the itch, I inhaled. I visualized myself grabbing Nacho's remains and flinging them into the room where the piano war was happening. I'd follow on Nacho's heels, burst into the room, and yell, "Did you see that?"

Would the presence of a fake ghost, a practical joke haunting, be enough to make Abuelita and her sister knock it off? Could I scoop Nacho off the living room floor by his eye holes while we all laughed, glad that a dead dog sailing across plates of burnt gelatina had reminded us what bullshit family heirlooms are because bugs and bacteria will inherit every heirloom and its heir someday? Termites will shit the world's finest pianos. Even prime ministers' eyeballs will jelly.

Somebody was shouting. She sounded like a turkey ready to get it on.

Grandma B had had a relationship with a turkey. She met Grandpa in a park that had used to be penitentiary grounds. After dynamite leveled the prison, masons installed its fountains and cobblestone paths. Landscapers planted grass, shade trees, and shrubbery. American expats convened around the gargling water to talk shit about the war that had claimed their lungs, eyes, feet, legs, arms, hands, or sanity. Dad's dad wasn't exactly an expat, he'd come to Mexico intact to learn Spanish, and he was rubbing elbows with the American who still had arms, reminiscing about home, when a green-eyed Mexican girl approached him. In Spanish, she asked him, "What's your name?"

His name and hers are inconsequential. What matters is that she was fifteen and a native Spanish speaker. He was thirty-two and blonde enough to be an Aryan poster boy.

They married and worked on making babies in an apartment near the park. Grandpa got a job as a livestock inspector, checking animals for foot and mouth disease. One afternoon, he came home from work with a turkey.

Its unpredictable wattle charmed Grandma B. His cocky, yet cognitively challenged walk, charmed her as well.

"Moco," she decided. "This bird's name is Moco."

Grandma B squatted beside Moco and stroked his wing. He followed her around the house as she swept. He groomed himself while she painted her fingernails red. He napped with her everyday at two o'clock. Bird and teen woman dreamt near an open window, basking.

In November, Grandpa told Grandma B, "Go to the market. Pick up stale bread, potatoes, carrots, and celery."

Grandma B carried shopping bags to the market, bought requested groceries, and came home.

"Mo-co!" she called. She heard no bird claws clacking against tiles. No flapping. No gobbling. No clucking. Nothing Turkish. "Moco!" she cried again.

Hearing commotion in the kitchen, she hurried to it. From kitchen doorway, she observed Grandpa from the waist up. He was standing at the chopping block, wearing his undershirt. His Polish face mashed with concentration and pleasure as he nestled bird corpse into tray. On the wood beside it, a bloody feather mountain. Beside this pillow stuffing, Moco's head. His regretful eyes looked at Grandma B. Had Marie Antoinette's eyes been open? Jayne Mansfield's?

"Assassin!" screamed Grandma B.

Unshaken, Grandpa looked up at her. In Spanish, he flatly announced, "Feliz Thanksgiving."

III. Behoove

Los cochinitos ya están en la cama
muchos besitos les dió su mamá
y calientitos todos con pijama
dentro de un rato los tres roncarán

Uno soñaba que era rey
y de momento quiso un pastel

su gran ministro hizo traer
500 paseteles nomás para el

> *Uno soñaba que en el mar*
> *en una lancha iba a remar*
> *mas de repente al embarcar*
> *se cayó de la cama y se puso a llorar...*

I sit beneath that dining room light bulb that keeps fizzling out. It makes sizzling sounds as it dies and reincarnates. My forearms press against cloth placemat. Holly patterns repeat across it. Perfect for August. I'm still staring at the piano.

Raindrops plink against hollow roof. Dull bullets from a failing revolution. I look to my left through the windows at the backyard. Darkness obscures white lilies and moss that grows wherever it feels like. Rancid newspaper piles and empty birdcages stacked against glass. Birds tweet somewhere.

Abuelito liked to sit on the chair against the window closest to me, the one by the empty easel. He'd cross his legs in ladylike fashion so that you could see his trouser socks and hungry ankles. A beige dot moves in the air there. I peer at it. It hovers above the chairs' twine seat. I inch my eyes closer as lights flicker and thunderclaps strengthen the cliché.

My head keeps moving closer so that I can get a better look at the mosquito or gnat blurring in figure eights. My neck keeps craning and craning till I have to stop or I will get a Moco neck. The thing isn't a gnat. It's not a mosquito ready to suck blood from gringa eye. What waves is a solitary hand that's been buried. Nobody's attached to it. Liver spots dapple its skin, and its fingers gnarl with hate and wisdom. Its knuckles are knobs that don't open a thing. The hand is so desiccated it's almost a monkey's paw, and it gestures over and over. It gestures universally. The gesture speaks, and the gesture writes, and the gesture writhes. It writes for those who can, can't, and would prefer not to. It writes for those who won't, and it writes for those who will never say, "Never say never." Never say never say never.

Go away. Leave. Get out. Shut the door. Did you forget something?
Human fingers curl in towards the palm and uncurl, pointing at the door.
Inhuman fingers curl in towards the palm and uncurl, pointing at the door.
This is not a feminine hand.
This is not a masculine hand.
This is a hand saying goodbye to its humanity.

This is a hand that wants you to leave. Take the rest of your life with
you. Shut the door. Inhale every sound. Taste everything that trembles
beneath the rabbit on the moon. Dunk it in milk first, like a child drowning
un puerquito de piloncillo in a glass of hot chocolate.

puerquitos de piloncillo puerquitos de piloncillo puerquitos de pilonicillo
little piggy cookies little piggy cookies little piggy cookies
sugar cane sugar cane sugar cane
behoove behoove behoove
hoof hoof hoof
bienvenido
a
la
muerte
.

(Be Hooves

Los cochinitos ya están en la cama
muchos besitos les dió su mamá
y calientitos todos con pijama
dentro de un rato los tres roncarán

Uno soñaba que era rey
y de momento quiso un pastel
su gran ministro hizo traer
500 paseteles nomás para el

Otro soñaba que en el mar
en una lancha iba a remar
mas de repente al embarcar
se cayó de la cama y se puso a llorar

Los cochinitos ya están en la cama
muchos besitos les dió su mamá
y calientitos todos con pijama
dentro de un rato los tres roncarán

El más pequeno de los tres
Un cochinito lindo y cortés
ése soñaba con trabajar
Para ayudar a su pobre mamá

Y asi soñando sin despertar
Los cochinitos pueden jugar
Ronca que ronca y vuelta a roncar
Al país de los sueños se van a pasear.

Perhaps this lullaby belongs to your childhood landscape, too. If you had an abuelita who painted your portrait in oils and who died with bedsores the color and consistency of key lime pies, she may have croaked it to you while she sketched your profile. If you're gringich and have no clue what this lullaby evokes, it's simple and stupid. Three piglets snuggle in bed. Their mother has kissed them goodnight. Snouts are snoring. Their onomatopoeia sounds like *me-me-me-me-me…*

As he dreams of being king, one piglet's mouth waters. He orders a grand minister to feed him, and he pigs out on a bazillion cakes. Wuss piglet dreams he's stepping into a rowboat. Instead, he rolls out of bed, smacks dirt floor, and cries. The runt is Tío Miguel. Self-effacing and good. Practically a woman. He works to help his mother. He empties all the pesos from his pockets, places the on a painter's palette, and slides it towards her. He tells Abuelita, "Use this money to buy yarn, turpentine, oils, chewing gum, papaya, and adult diapers. I will never abandon you. If needed, I will chew your food and spit it down your throat. I love you."

The pigs dream, and the pigs snore. Pigs frolic in the Land of Nod. The Land of Nod opens into a Mexican village you can't get to by foot, train, or cruise ship. You've got to be born there. Its people are hungry.

To nourish themselves, some of the hungry lick the walls. Others dig the dead out of their graves and boil their bones into broth. Heretics hunt and broil the sacred hummingbird. They fry tiny omelets out of its eggs. Who's got the tiny bacon?

In this very village, a newlywed is traveling to the well. Her skin gives off that new mother glow. She's balancing a clay jug on her shoulder. She has left her baby in its crib. It's screaming for her like crazy, but she knows she has to teach the baby that every time it screams, she can't come running. She is Ferberizing the thing. She steps beyond her creature's wails. And keeps walking.

The lady slides one of her pompis onto the bricks. She leans. She skims her jug along the water and coolness whooshes in. Water refreshes the clay, the smell reminds the lady of when rain first touches the dirt. She hoists the container back onto her shoulder and doesn't spill any walking back to her house.

Good. The baby has sshhed.

At the threshold, the lady sets down her jug beside her husband's pickaxe. She tiptoes to reward the baby for its silence. Creeping into the room, she finds only a blanket and cradle. Where is the baby? Her titty hangs out and ready. Its two hairs stiffen like cockroach antennae.

She glances at the window. Dark mud streaks the sill. Matching mud streaks the dirt floor as much as dirt can streak dirt. Carambas. This baby really learned its lesson. It's so silent it vanished.

Somewhere, a butterfly is yawning. The mother tears out of her house with that tit flopping like a fish that'll do anything to get back into water but knows it'll die out here with us. She wails, and her wail would terrify anyone who could hear it, but it lacks an audience. Every house the mother screams past is overgrown by greasewood. Collapsed roofs scatter across dirt floors. Doors hang open eyelidishly. Only burrowing earthworms hear the muffled wails. Have you heard this woman's wails on certain nights? Imagine the most horrible wail a woman could release from her body. Please, really try to imagine this or maybe you don't have to. Maybe this wail is already part of you: *My baby... where is my baby?*

The mother tears through her village with that tit flopping out. She tears past the witch doctor's hut, the rectory, the chapel, the post office that has no point (nobody writes letters anymore), the mercantile, and the tavern. Bandits' voices carry out its windows. Five of them huddle around a table, commiserating around a clay pitcher of pulque, but they are plotting to rob gold, gold from a ghost. They have no interest in babies unless they've swallowed gold, so they're not our culprits.

The mother and her tit continue their spree. They tear past the mayor's house and past the bordello's pink front door, and on the house of ill repute's whitewashed but mossiest wall, the mother sees a pile. Snoozing swine make up this heap, they're curled into and around each other's mauve bodies, so many potential pork chops, so much meat that can't nourish an orthodox Hebrew. The cutest piglet is swaddled in her son's blanket. The blankey used to be white before she went to fetch water.

Pig's in a red blanket. The sight drains the final drops of sanity from the mother's mind, and she tiptoes to the animal pile and crouches near blood-stained snouts. A sow snores onto her wild nipple.

Its hairs perk, antennas

Baby's breath)

Acknowledgments

Muchas grassy ass to RADAR PRODUCTIONS for giving me places to write and stages and places to read on, to Kevin Sampsell for being my literary jockstrap (ultra supportive), Wendy C. Ortiz for being a bomb ass lady, the Tostis for being my second family, all the ghosts who visit me and give me inspirayshuns, my pretty feminist momma and handsome feminist dad, my bro and sis yaz and dave, my gorgeous Uncle Henry, my abuelita and abuelito for indoctrinating me in art, tatiana de la tierra for being my queer elder, Thais Jones for being my white girl, Griselda Suarez por ser mi jota y guayaba, Jen Joseph for championing this weirdness, and TJ for being such a TJ.